THE Seventh Princess

Nick Sullivan

A LITTLE APPLE PAPERBACK

SCHOLASTIC INC.
New York Toronto London Auckland Sydney
Mexico City New Delhi Hong Kong

ISBN 0-439-26007-8

Published by Scholastic Inc., 555 Broadway, New York, NY 10012,
by arrangement with Scholastic Cananda Ltd.

12 11 10 9 8 7 6 5 4 3 2 1 1 2 3 4 5 6/0

Printed in the U.S.A. 40

First Scholastic Inc. printing, May 2001

Table of Contents

1
An unusual journey

On a cold, foggy morning in the month of November Jennifer sat by herself in the big yellow schoolbus. It was the worst of days. Carol sat across the aisle, not speaking to Jennifer. Erin was there too, talking with Carol. No one was speaking to Jennifer today. Not even Jason, who would speak to anybody. Jennifer could not understand all this silence, but if she had been able to see her own face she would not have been so puzzled, for even she would have been a little afraid of the fearsome scowl that curled her lip, darkened her eyes and creased her forehead with long, deep furrows as she thought about her homework.

Jennifer always did her homework, always neatly and always well—she was very proud of that. But on Friday Mrs. Ritchie had told the class to write a composition called "My Strangest Dream" over the weekend, and here it was Monday and Jennifer had not written a word.

How could I? she thought miserably. I never *have* any dreams! At least, if I do I don't remember them.

She tried to put it out of her mind by looking out the window. They were just coming to her favourite part of the ride to school—down the hill to the river, across the old bridge, then up again along the winding road through the woods that came almost to the edge of town.

And such woods! Shadowy and mysterious they were, even in daylight: wet, tangled and thorny by the riverbank, drier and more open as they climbed the hill to the road. But even there no shaft of sunlight could pierce the thick roof of branches high above.

As the old bus rattled across the bridge and began to make its way up into this strange kingdom of trees, Jennifer closed her eyes tightly for a moment and let her thoughts wander. Maybe there were places here where no one had ever been, places which no eyes had ever looked upon. What creatures lurked here? What mysteries did the dark woods conceal? What unseen watchers might there be, even now, staring from some treetop hiding place as the yellow bus rolled by? Elves? Goblins? Lumbering, stone-hearted trolls?

A sudden jolt nearly threw Jennifer from her seat and she opened her eyes with a start. Then she opened them wider and threw her hand to her mouth to stifle a scream. Something was terribly wrong.

She was riding in a carriage, a big, beautiful carriage with sides and roof of solid oak carved with curious designs. She sat on a blue satin cushion on a broad bench, with more cushions behind her and about her on both sides. There was another bench across from her, but she was alone. She could hear the rumbling of wooden wheels on dirt and the thudding hooves of trotting horses as the carriage bumped along. A lace curtain was drawn across the window to one side of her.

Her heart thumping, Jennifer pulled it aside. The forest was still there, with its secrets and shadows. Now more than ever she sensed unseen eyes staring from the gloom. She did not feel that they were friendly. Of the big yellow schoolbus there was no sign.

She dragged herself away from the window and sank back into the soft pile of cushions, too astonished even to be very frightened. What had happened?

Her first thought was that it was all a trick, a huge, complicated joke arranged by her friends. But that made no sense at all.

What then? Had she gone mad? She didn't *feel* mad, but that didn't necessarily mean anything. Jennifer shut her eyes tightly and recited the seven times table out loud, having a vague notion that this was something no mad person could possibly do. Then, just to make sure, she tried the eight and nine times tables as well. No, she decided, she hadn't gone mad.

She opened her eyes again, cautiously, one at a time, hoping that just possibly everything would be back to normal.

It wasn't.

She was beginning to feel really scared. What was

going on? It did no good to tell herself that the whole situation was impossible, for here she was right in the middle of it, impossible or not. Where was the bus? Where were her friends? Would she ever see them again?

It was crazy, it was horrible, it was as senseless as a bad dream!

Wait! That was it—a dream! Jennifer laughed out loud with relief. One minute she had been fretting about her homework, telling herself she never had dreams. The next minute she had shut her eyes—and then *this* had happened. It was too funny for words.

Well, it was nice to have that sorted out. The question was: what to do next? Jennifer was sure that if she just thought about it hard enough, or perhaps pinched herself a couple of times, she would wake up and find herself back in the real world. But why bother? Now that she knew what was happening it seemed a pity to spoil it. Much better to go along with it for a while, to see what strange and wonderful paths her dream would follow. After all, she was quite safe and really very comfortable, at least for the time being. She would be waking up in a few moments anyway, as soon as the bus pulled into the school yard.

She turned back to the window. The carriage was out of the forest now, and in every direction all that could be seen were wide fields of crops on neatly kept farms. Here and there were curious, brightly painted buildings—houses and barns, Jennifer supposed—with round walls and pointed roofs. Once or twice she thought she glimpsed people and animals far away in the distance, but it was difficult to be sure.

Oddly, it did not feel at all like November anymore. The fog and clouds of the morning had vanished and a hot sun shone from a clear blue sky. The wide fields of dark green corn and the garden plots bursting with row upon row of leafy vegetables seemed to show that in this dream world it was barely midsummer, maybe early July. That alone was a good reason to stay dreaming a little while longer.

On an impulse Jennifer stood up and leaned her head out the window to see if she could catch sight of the driver. As she did so she discovered that she was travelling much faster than it had seemed from inside. There were four horses, all of pure white and all galloping in earnest. Her long golden hair streamed out behind her as she craned her neck to get a view of the driver's seat. But try as she might, she could not see around to the front of the coach. Disappointed, she left the window and returned to her seat.

By now she seemed to have been in the carriage for hours. Comfortable as it was, the dream was becoming tedious. Again Jennifer considered waking herself up. But before she could make up her mind to do so, her idle glance fell on a drawer that was built into the front of the bench opposite her.

She reached for the heavy brass handle, looking around nervously as she did so, half expecting someone to appear suddenly and scold her for prying. But after all, she thought, it is *my* dream. Why shouldn't I pry?

Satisfied with this reasoning, she slid the drawer open and found to her disappointment that it held nothing but clothes. On top was a pale yellow frock with a gold hem and flowers embroidered on the front. Beneath it, neatly folded, was a sky-blue satin cloak with a jewelled fastener. Near the back of the drawer was a pair of yellow knee stockings, and beside them a pair of slippers. These seemed to be made of solid silver, cushioned inside with velvet. Finally there was a small box, made of glass or crystal, which held a necklace of pure white pearls.

Ordinarily Jennifer was not the sort of person who greatly cared for frocks and silver slippers, or even pearl necklaces. But this was a kind of special occasion, she felt, and besides, there was nothing else to do. So, after looking around once again just to make sure that no one was watching, she took off her jeans and her shirt, folded them carefully into the drawer and slipped on the yellow dress.

Strangely enough it fitted her perfectly; it seemed almost to have been made for her. Next she tried on the stockings and the shoes. The shoes were rather uncomfortable, being silver, but they weren't as heavy as she had expected. Then she fastened the pearls around her neck, put on the sky-blue cloak with the jewelled clasp and shut the drawer with her own clothes in it, feeling very naughty and rather grand at the same time.

Hardly had she sat down again, though, than she realized with a start that the carriage had slowed down. Turning to the window, she looked out and found herself on a street in a great city. It was filled with people dressed in strange costumes, and lined with quaint-looking shops and little stalls selling, besides food and other commonplace things, many strange articles that Jennifer could not identify.

A stream of carriages was passing by in the other direction, though none was as large or luxurious as the one in which she was riding. To Jennifer's astonishment, everyone who caught sight of her peering out from behind the lace curtains (and they all seemed to be looking her way) would stand very respectfully facing her and bow low as she passed by.

It's these clothes, she thought in sudden panic. They're mistaking me for someone else. What will they do when they find out? I'd better change back right now!

But at that very moment the carriage turned through an ornate gate onto a broad avenue. Ahead Jennifer could see a huge palace with high towers and spires, fountains on the lawn in front and a guard of resplendently-uniformed soldiers lined up on the steps leading to the doors. There the carriage stopped. It was too late to get back into her old clothes now.

The carriage door swung open and a tall man with dark, stern eyes strode towards her with his hand outstretched.

"I-I-I'm sorry about the clothes!" Jennifer stammered, her face scarlet. "Really I am! I know I shouldn't be wearing them."

But the man appeared not to hear her.

"Welcome!" he said in a voice that seemed to come from the soles of his red leather boots. He bowed solemnly even as he helped her down onto the grass. "It is pleasant to see your Highness looking so well."

2
The palace

Your Highness! This dream was certainly becoming more interesting! What did this man take her for, a queen or something? Jennifer tried to put on her most ladylike manner.

"Thank you very much," she replied. "And who may you be, sir?" She almost added, "And who may *I* be, for that matter?" but thought better of it.

"I am Duke Rinaldo, your Highness," the man told her gravely. "Lord High Chancellor of your Highness's most loyal realm of Eladeria. Amongst other duties."

"Congratulations," said Jennifer, although it didn't seem quite the correct reply. Then she said, "Where is the driver of my carriage, if you please? I would like to see that he or she is rewarded for my very comfortable journey."

Actually she only wanted to see the driver's face, just to satisfy her earlier curiosity, but the idea of royally rewarding someone was pleasing too.

"Driver, your Highness?" inquired Rinaldo, a ghost of a smile playing on his thin lips. "Did your Highness not know? There *was* no driver." He held up a long, bony finger, pointing behind her. "And see—"

Following his gesture, Jennifer turned around and gasped. There was no sign of carriage or horses to be seen.

"But how—That is, I should have heard—"

She looked about her at the faces of the many splendid attendants standing nearby. None of them seemed aware that anything out of the ordinary had taken place.

"All will be explained, your Highness," Rinaldo assured her. "But first, if your Highness will permit me to accompany her into the palace?"

Despite the Lord Chancellor's courteous words and attentive manner Jennifer could not help feeling that he was not in the least concerned for her, that his friendliness and courtesy were like a mask that he could put on or take off at his own convenience. Was it only her imagination that made his narrow eyes seem to glint so coldly? What would he do if I said no? she wondered. Would he still be so kind?

"I really don't feel like being indoors on such a beautiful day," she said aloud. "I think I'll go for a walk instead, Duke. Perhaps I'll see you later on."

"May I remind your Highness," Rinaldo protested smoothly, "that the whole court is assembled in the Great Hall to greet your arrival, and that it would be unseemly to keep the lords and ladies waiting? And surely your Highness wishes to see the King, who even now lies gravely ill in his chambers?"

"I didn't ask for anyone to greet me," retorted Jennifer. "Let them wait a little longer if they choose, or let them do whatever they want. And if the King is sick, well, I'm sorry, but I'm no doctor."

There was a low murmur of astonishment from the guards and attendants standing nearby. Rinaldo quieted them with a wave of his hand. Then he leaned down so close to Jennifer that their noses almost touched, still smiling politely.

"If you know what's good for you," he said under his breath, "you'll come with me now, little fool, and make no more trouble. Or later you'll regret it most painfully, I promise you!"

Jennifer gulped. Well, she thought, at least I know where I stand now! But I wish I was standing somewhere else!

"If your Highness will take my arm?" Rinaldo went on in a voice that the attendants could hear. "I know the King is awaiting you anxiously."

Uncomfortable as she felt walking on Duke Rinaldo's arm, Jennifer found more than enough to distract her as they made their way up the cobbled path to the palace steps.

The grounds around were full of people of all ranks and stations, from haughty nobles with ermine robes and silk slippers to gardeners and groundskeepers in simple work clothes of cotton. The latter seemed to be very busy attending to their work of weeding flower beds or trimming hedges, while the nobles appeared to have little better to do than stand about with a bored air chatting idly with their fellows. It was vexing to Jennifer that she could see little of their faces, for it seemed that the moment she caught anyone's eye that person would bow so low that only the crown of his head was visible.

Through the crowds of people tame animals wandered at will: ungainly pink flamingos, strutting peacocks, a pair of giraffes, an elephant and a great many dogs of every size and colour.

On the palace steps, which were built of marble and stood out from the huge building itself in a wide half-circle, a triple row of guards stood stiffly to attention at either side. Their armour was polished till it hurt the eyes; their long straight swords hung from their hips in ruby-studded scabbards. The moment Jennifer set her foot on each step of the broad stairway, the guards on that step would lift their swords high into the air and cry "Hail!" in such deafening voices that her head was aching long before she reached the top.

At last, though, they came to the great double doors. At a sign from Duke Rinaldo these were flung open with a flourish of trumpets from heralds standing nearby. The procession moved inside with Jennifer at the front, trying to look more royal than she felt.

She found herself in the Great Hall. The huge room had a floor of inlaid marble and a domed roof that seemed impossibly high. The tapestried walls were lined with page-boys, ladies-in-waiting and innumerable other courtiers, all bowing and curtseying towards her at once.

Before Jennifer had had time to take this in properly, however, there was a commotion from one side and in burst a figure like none she had ever seen. It was a dwarf, no taller than Jennifer herself, dressed in the pied costume of a court jester with cap, bells and huge pointed slippers turned up at the toes. This strange creature tumbled into the hall in such a flurry of cartwheels and pratfalls that Jennifer could not help but laugh, especially when he somersaulted through midair to land at her very feet, all but knocking her down.

"Insolent dog!" Rinaldo growled. "You shall be whipped for this! Yes, and you shall sleep in the stables for a week!"

"He shall do no such thing!" exclaimed Jennifer, deciding that she had better take charge of this dream before it got completely out of hand. "No, he should be rewarded rather!"

She turned to the small figure of the jester with interest. The dwarf had fallen back a few paces and was regarding her keenly with his bright eyes.

"What is your name, sir?" Jennifer inquired politely. "What shall I call you?"

At the word "sir" Rinaldo cringed, but the dwarf ignored him.

"Why, Highness," he replied in a sing-song voice, "my name is Samson. But as for what you shall call me, that is up to you. Insolent Dog is popular this season. Also Peabrain, Crookface, Worm, Stinkweed and Monkey." He nodded at Rinaldo. "My Lord the Chancellor could doubtless suggest more names, Highness, if those do not please you."

Rinaldo glowered and roughly drew Samson aside by the shoulder.

"When I have done with you, fool of a Fool," he

hissed softly, "your names shall be Gap-Tooth, One-Eye and Peg-Leg. I know your mind, lack-witted jester. You seek to use the Princess against me, hoping at the same time that she will protect you. Simpleton! What do I care for any feeble scheme of yours? And who will protect you when she is gone?"

"Why do you whisper, my Lord?" returned the jester in a voice loud enough for Jennifer to hear. "In the presence of her Highness you should display better manners! And do not seek to bully me as you bully others. For all the beatings I have suffered at your command, Rinaldo, for all the days without food and the sleepless nights in the stables, yes, and for all your insults and mockery you shall yet pay!"

Jennifer scowled. So that was how Rinaldo enforced his authority! With threats, with beatings, with starvation and other cruel treatment. It was not as though Samson could possibly be any real danger to Rinaldo, she thought. It was obvious that the Chancellor had all the power. Instantly she made up her mind that if there were any opportunity for her to help the jester she would take it.

But Rinaldo himself was quite unmoved by the jester's outburst. With a sneer twisting his thin lips he turned away, ending the exchange. He made a small signal with his right hand and at once two courtiers stepped forward, an old man and an old woman, stiff in their uncomfortable finery. They stopped before Jennifer and bowed.

"Your Highness," Rinaldo said, "permit me to introduce Duke Hugo, Lord High Steward of the Palace, and Dame Isobel, First Lady of your Highness's Chambers. They will attend you until it is time for your audience with the King. And now, if your Highness will forgive me, I have other matters to attend to."

Without waiting for a reply, Rinaldo withdrew. Jennifer was left in the centre of the great room with only Samson and the two old courtiers beside her.

"Well," she said, looking to each of them in turn, "where next?"

3
The Princess Miranda

For a moment following Rinaldo's departure no one spoke. Then, "That is entirely up to your Highness," Duke Hugo began in a reedy, quavering voice. "Perhaps a rest after your fatiguing journey? Or a tour of the palace and its grounds? There is much of historical and artistic interest that your Highness might be pleased to see."

"No," said Jennifer apologetically, "I don't think I'm quite ready for a tour yet, Duke Hugo. As a matter of fact, what I'd really like is a bit of lunch if it wouldn't be too much trouble. I can fix myself a sandwich or something if you'll just show me where I can find the kitchen."

"Your Highness fix her own lunch?" Hugo's tone was shocked and Dame Isobel turned deathly pale and had to hold on to the Duke for support. Suddenly both of them threw themselves down and put their heads to the floor at Jennifer's feet.

"Alas, I am nothing more than an old fool!" Hugo moaned. "Of course your Highness is famished. How did I not think of it? It is unforgivable! Do not trouble to call the guards, your Highness. I shall go to the dungeons this minute and lock myself in!"

And with these words the pitiful old steward arose and would really have taken himself off to the dungeons had Jennifer not caught him by the arm to comfort him.

"There, there, Hugo!" she said gently. "I'm sure you've had a lot on your mind with a royal visit to get ready for and all. Anyone could have made the same mistake. And besides, if you go to the dungeons, who will see that I get my lunch?"

Hugo brightened somewhat at this.

"That is true, your Highness," he said gratefully. "I had not thought of that. If it please your Highness, then, I will have a little something sent up to your chambers as soon as it can be arranged. If your Highness will excuse me?"

Jennifer nodded and Hugo went off as rapidly as his stiff clothes and his dignity would permit.

"Good," Jennifer said to Dame Isobel, who was still in shock at the thought of royalty preparing its own lunch, and to Samson, who had watched the whole scene with a twinkle of wry amusement in his eyes. "Now that that's settled, will you guide me to my chamber please, Dame Isobel? And you, Samson, do come with us."

They travelled up a long corridor lined with dark and musty portraits ("Your ancestors!" Samson told Jennifer with a strange laugh) which led to another chamber, not so large or bright as the first, with arched passageways opening from it in many directions.

Down one of these Dame Isobel guided them, past doorways on the left and on the right, and across more passages, till suddenly they came to a small door which opened onto a sunny and spacious courtyard.

In it was a pool fed by a fountain in the shape of a miniature spouting whale. Fawns gambolled on the grass nearby, coming at times to drink at the edge of the pool. From a window high overhead came the music of lute and recorder playing a stately air with a long-ago sound to it. It was so sweet that Jennifer longed to be able to stay and hear more.

"Such a dream!" she sighed. "It would be a pity to wake up now!"

"A dream, Highness?" asked Samson sharply. "Is that what you think? Well, well! Wake up while you can, Highness, if it's a dream. Aye, I should wake up myself, maybe, and be a dwarf no more!"

Before Jennifer had time to ask what he meant by this curious speech Dame Isobel beckoned them to a door on the far side of the courtyard. It opened into yet another hall, this one brightly lit by torches set into brass sockets high up the old stone walls. She guided them to a staircase leading away on one side of the hall, its stone steps thickly carpeted. The stairs were broad enough for the three to walk abreast, and they wound up and about till they gained another corridor, wider and grander than the others. Dame Isobel led them as far as the third door on the left and stopped.

"Your Highness's chambers," she said, and opened the door for the others to enter.

Inside was not the simple bedroom Jennifer had been expecting, but an apartment royally furnished: a large sitting room at the front, a bedroom almost as big behind it, a tiled bathroom with a silver washstand and a huge copper bathtub, and several smaller rooms off to the sides. On a table in the centre of the sitting room was a golden tray loaded with delicacies of food and drink, with Duke Hugo standing beside it watching nervously as Jennifer approached.

"I hope all will be to your Highness's satisfaction," he said at once. "If there had been more time—"

"More time!" exclaimed Jennifer. The smell of roast chicken rising from a covered platter on the tray reminded her sharply how hungry she was. There was also a dish of fresh fruit topped by a huge bunch of green grapes, no fewer than three desserts, and pitchers of milk, water and mead. "More time!" she said again. "Goodness, Hugo, how on earth did you get here before us with all this? It seems like magic!"

"Alas, no magic," said Hugo, "else would your Highness be lunching on better fare than this. But in truth I came as swiftly as these old legs would bear me, your Highness. And I may say that none know the short and secret ways of this palace better than I do—save Master Samson perhaps."

"Stop apologizing all the time, Hugo, really!" said Jennifer. "I haven't seen a meal like this since Christmas! But I can't possibly eat it all myself. Sit down, all three of you, and help me."

"Eat with your Highness?" Hugo was aghast.

"Surely your Highness jests."

"No," replied Jennifer, "that's Samson's job. Stop fussing, Hugo, and sit down. Here, have a leg of chicken. You look as though you don't eat enough."

With that, Jennifer sat down herself and set to, very pleased with the way things were going. Not only was the food delicious, but scolding adults was fun too, although you had to do it gently, she reminded herself. Old Hugo looked as though he would burst into tears if she were too hard on him.

When they were all comfortably full she leaned back in her chair and turned to Samson.

"Now," she said firmly, "I have some questions that I want you to answer." The jester nodded expectantly. "First," Jennifer went on, "the name of this country is, uh, Alo—, no, Elo—"

"Eladeria," Samson said. "And this is the capital city, Tumbol."

"Eladeria. Right. And I am—"

"Her Royal Highness, Princess Miranda," said the jester, seemingly not at all astonished that the Princess did not know her own name. "Only daughter of King Theobald the Fourth, Monarch of Eladeria, Lord Protector of the Eastern Marches, Akond of Simmery and Swat, *etcetera, etcetera.*"

"All right," said Jennifer, letting this sink in for a moment. "Princess Miranda. I like that! Only daughter of the King, you say?"

"Only *living* daughter, I should have said," Samson told her, looking rather uncomfortable. "So far as we know."

Somehow Jennifer didn't like the sound of that so much.

"Oh!" she went on after a moment's thought. "And has the King any sons?"

"He *had* one," replied the dwarf, looking even more uncomfortable. "Prince Corbold. He vanished mysteriously on a hunting journey some seven years ago and naught has been seen of him since. It is feared he must be dead."

"Oh, I *am* sorry!" said Jennifer. "How the poor King must feel! And now tell me of Duke Rinaldo."

"Ah, Rinaldo!" muttered Samson rather grimly. "Of him there is much one could say. He was a great warrior in his youth, your Highness, and travelled far, and saw many strange things, if rumours are to be believed. Aye, and he knows much that is hidden from ordinary folk, it is said. As for his duties, as Lord High Chancellor Rinaldo makes the laws, and enforces them, and punishes those who break them. What is more, he does much else that King Theobald would do were he well. For example, he commands the army and the navy, treats with foreign princes, levies and collects taxes, oversees the building of—"

"I think I'm starting to get the picture," Jennifer said, interrupting. "But you say the King is sick? Rinaldo mentioned it too. What's the matter with him?"

The dwarf threw his hands into the air. "Yes, what *is* the matter with him?" he repeated. "A very good question."

Dame Isobel spoke up unexpectedly. "It was some years ago, your Highness—in fact not long after we lost good Prince Corbold—that the King fell into a terrible illness from which he has been very slow to recover, though the best doctors and herb-healers in the Kingdom have attended him. Ever since, he has spent most of his time in his bed, hardly opening his eyes or stirring a muscle, and only Duke Rinaldo can talk to him or persuade him to put his pen to the proclamations that Rinaldo writes in his name." Isobel's eyes burned with a strange, angry light as she continued in a voice that dropped to a hoarse whisper, "It is said that witchcraft has robbed him of his will!"

"Witchcraft! And Rinaldo again! That man seems to be in everything!" She turned to Samson. "Earlier today Rinaldo said I was to have an audience with the King. Do you know anything about that?"

"Yes," said Samson. "That is the usual way of it. And listen. There's something you should—"

Before he could finish there was a loud rap at the door, and without awaiting a reply Rinaldo himself strode in, a herald and a guard at his back.

"His Majesty awaits, your Highness," he announced in a voice as cold and brittle as ice. "Will your Highness please come with me?"

4

A visit to the King

Jennifer rose at once.

"Of course," she said to Rinaldo. "I will come immediately. Samson, if you have no other duties will you await me here? There is more I would like to ask you. Dame Isobel, Duke Hugo, thank you both for your kindness. I know you have many other things to do, so I won't ask you to stay. But I hope to see you again soon."

All three bowed. But Duke Rinaldo, who had been tapping his foot impatiently all the while, said, "Come, your Highness! The summons of a king brooks no delay!"

With that he took Jennifer by the arm and led her out into the corridor. They took a different direction from the one she had come by earlier, so Jennifer was at once lost. Rinaldo strode along without speaking and at such a pace that it was all she could do to keep up. The herald and the guard who had come with Rinaldo followed a few paces behind them.

Again the way led through great halls and wide corridors that seemed to go on forever, up and down staircases and occasionally through small courtyards, though none so beautiful as the one Jennifer had crossed earlier.

At last they came to a narrow corridor with no doors, save one at the very end. Heavily-armed guards were lined up stiffly on either side. It reminded Jennifer more of a prison than a king's chambers. She said nothing, however, and neither did Rinaldo until they were nearly at the end of the corridor. Then he leaned over and whispered in her ear.

"Remember, little fool," he said, "you are entering the presence of the King. He is not well, you realize, and may say or do strange things. Pay them no mind! He is a king, and as far above a simple child like you as you are above an ant! Do not speak unless he asks you a direct question, and then answer as quickly and as clearly as you can. And always say 'Your Majesty.' Do you understand?"

Jennifer nodded.

"Good. See that you do as I say or it will be the worse for you."

Rinaldo's guard stepped forward to open the door for them. The herald took a pace through the doorway and cried, "The Princess Miranda and the Lord High Chancellor, Duke Rinaldo, at King Theobald's command!"

Another herald inside the room responded, "By the King's leave, enter and be welcome!"

The chambers of the King were even larger than Jennifer's own, and more grandly though less comfortably furnished. The first room was filled with the usual assortment of nobility and attendants, all bowing and bobbing at once until Duke Rinaldo ordered them out the door with an impatient wave of his hand. He crossed the room to check that the King was alone in his chamber, then beckoned Jennifer forward. The guard and the herald were left to stand watch at the door.

Jennifer gulped. She had never met a king before and did not know what to expect. She approached timidly and followed Rinaldo into the bedchamber. At once she saw the King, apparently asleep in his great bed, a heavy golden crown on a small table beside him, and she could not hold back a gasp of astonishment and pity.

"Silence!" whispered Rinaldo fiercely, but Jennifer scarcely heard him.

King Theobald was an old man, though Jennifer guessed he looked older than he really was. His long white hair came down untidily on both sides of a deeply furrowed face that must once have been handsome; his snowy beard was matted and untrimmed. He was lying on his back wearing a coarse nightgown of white cloth turned grey with age and long use. His hands outstretched upon the coverlet were veiny and as thin as his haggard face. He did not look like a king.

Theobald did not stir when they entered. Rinaldo, on whose face Jennifer could see nothing but contempt for the frail old man, crossed to the bedside and whispered something into his ear. Jennifer could not make out what the Chancellor was saying, but it went on for some time, his voice rising and falling as if he were chanting, or uttering an incantation.

At last the King's eyes opened, though they were filmed and bleary, and he turned his head to Rinaldo without lifting it from the pillow.

"Rinaldo," he said in a voice drained of strength. "Most loyal Rinaldo. How good of you to come! How fares the Kingdom? Are the people happy? I must get up soon, Rinaldo, and see how things are, I really must. It isn't fair to leave everything to you. When I am well again. Yes, next week perhaps."

"The Kingdom prospers, your Majesty," responded Rinaldo, "though of course the people miss their King. But look, your Majesty, I have brought someone to see you."

The King's old eyes turned to follow the Chancellor's pointing finger. After roving aimlessly around the room for a few moments, his gaze found Jennifer.

"What? What?" he croaked. "Who is that? Not the Queen, surely? Not my own Rebecca? No. She is too young, I think. Much too young."

"Peace, your Majesty," said Rinaldo. "The Queen is dead, long dead. Do you not remember? No, it is the Princess Miranda, Majesty. She has come."

"What, so soon? Has she come so soon? It has not been a twelvemonth surely, Rinaldo? Not yet?"

"It has, my Liege. You must sign the proclamation."

"Must I?" asked the King. "Yes, I suppose I must. How many will this be, Rinaldo? So young! How many? Three, is it? Is she the third?"

"The seventh, your Majesty."

"The seventh? The *seventh?*" The old King rose

up on his elbows and clenched his fists till the knuckles whitened, seized by a sudden fit of anger. Then he sank back wearily. "Will she never be done?" he asked in a hollow voice. "Will the old hag never be done? But tell me, Rinaldo, how long till the moon is full? Two weeks? Three? Has she yet a little while?"

"It waxes even now, your Majesty. In five nights the moon will be full."

"Five nights! Poor child! You will see that she is well treated, Rinaldo? She will have every luxury?"

"She will be treated like a princess, my Liege. Of course. But come. Your Majesty is tiring. You must sign the proclamation."

So saying, he drew a parchment scroll from within the folds of his robe and opened it out for the King to see. He brought a quill and an ink bottle from a nearby table, dipped the pen and placed it in the King's trembling hand. Theobald's eyes flickered over the document without seeming to understand what it said. Finally he brought the quill down on a blank space near the bottom of the parchment and, in writing that trembled with his hand, scratched the words *Theobald Rex*.

Spent with the effort, he sank back onto the pillow once again. It seemed to Jennifer that he had fallen back to sleep, for his eyes closed and his head rolled to one side. Her heart went out to the frail old man. Hardly knowing what she did or why, she hurried to his side, knelt by him and kissed him gently on the cheek. Rinaldo tapped his foot angrily, but she ignored him.

Suddenly the King's hand came up to grip her

shoulder, his eyes flickered open and he whispered urgently in her ear, so softly that she could barely make out his words. "The Paladian Scroll, child, the Paladian Scroll! Find it! Use it! Your only chance!" A sudden gleam had brightened his pale eyes. His body tensed as though he were struggling with an invisible enemy. With a last effort he breathed, "Beware Rinaldo! Beware him!"

Then his grip on her shoulder relaxed and his eyes, once more dull, slowly closed. In a moment he was fast asleep.

Jennifer straightened and turned to the Chancellor. There was a question in his eyes that she did not want to answer.

He said harshly, "Come, he will say no more today," and led her from the chambers.

In the corridor Rinaldo hurried Jennifer past the guards almost at a trot. "What did he say?" he demanded. "When you kissed him he spoke to you. I saw his lips move. Tell me, what did he say?"

Jennifer's heart was thumping but she tried to look calm.

"He said, 'Bless you, my child,'" she answered. "And something more, something about my frock, I think. I couldn't make out the words."

Rinaldo relaxed. "Very well then," he said with an evil smile. "That is most touching. 'Bless you, my child,' eh? A good joke!"

"What was that paper?" Jennifer asked, trying to ignore the Chancellor's manner. The words "Beware him!" were still echoing in her mind. "Did it have something to do with me?"

"Something to do with you? Ha-ha! Something to

do with you indeed, little fool. That was a Proclamation of Adoption." Rinaldo nodded to a guard. "Escort Princess Miranda back to her chambers," he ordered. "See that no harm befalls her."

He turned back to Jennifer. "Do you understand, your Highness? The King has adopted you. You are his daughter now. A real princess! Enjoy it while you may!"

And he strode away, laughing.

5
An expedition is planned

When she returned to her chambers Jennifer found Samson waiting for her as she had asked. He had found a lute somewhere and was playing quietly to himself when she came in, but he put the instrument aside at once and waited in silence for her to settle down on a couch, an uncommonly serious expression on his comical face.

"Highness? Did you see the King? How is his Majesty?"

"Yes, I saw him, Samson," she replied. "And he is very sick. At least that's how he seemed to me. And very strange too. But Samson, would you do me a favour?"

"Whatever your Highness asks."

"Well then, stop calling me your Highness, if you please," said Jennifer. "At least when we're alone. It makes me uncomfortable, all these titles and the bowing and scraping that goes on all the time. I suppose a real princess might not mind, but I'm just not used to it! My name is Jennifer. Would you please call me that?"

The jester grinned. "Gladly, Jennifer," he answered. "I am honoured. But do tell me of the King."

"Well, he was very old looking and very frail," said Jennifer. "And he seemed—Well, he wasn't himself, you know? I don't mean just that he was ill," she explained hastily. "I mean he *really* wasn't himself. It was as though he was a puppet and someone else was pulling the strings, if that makes any sense. And Samson, I think I know who that someone is."

"I can guess who you mean," muttered the jester darkly. "But go on. What did the King say?"

"Many things that made no sense to me," Jennifer said. "All about the full moon and the Queen—Rinaldo had to tell him the Queen was dead, by the way; the King had forgotten. And that I was the seventh—the seventh *what* I don't know. And something about an old hag and would she never be done."

Samson's eyes glinted at the mention of the old hag, but he said nothing.

"Then Rinaldo made the King sign a scroll," Jennifer went on. "Afterwards he said it was a Proclamation of Adoption and it made me the King's daughter. Do you know anything about that?"

"A little," the jester replied. "I was expecting it in any case. Was there anything else?"

"Let me see. The King asked Rinaldo to make sure I was well-treated and Rinaldo, of course, said that he would. And then there was one other thing I thought was very strange. After he had signed the scroll the King seemed to fall straight back to sleep, just as though he couldn't keep himself awake any longer after he had done what Rinaldo wanted of him. Poor man, he looked so weary and ill, just like a sick old grandfather. I felt so sorry for him I went over to his bed and kissed him on the cheek, though with him being asleep I don't suppose that made much sense."

"Certainly it did," Samson told her. "But what then?"

"Well, when I kissed him he came awake again. He grabbed me and it seemed for a moment he had escaped whatever it was that was controlling him. He whispered something in my ear, but it didn't make any sense to me."

The dwarf leaned forward eagerly. "Do you remember what it was?"

"I think so," answered Jennifer. "It was—"

"Wait, don't say it!" he hissed suddenly. "It is not wise to say too much within the palace walls—*his* spies are everywhere!" Then in a normal tone he went on, "Perhaps you would like to see the city, Jennifer. Tumbol is a very interesting place; you would find a tour educational, I am sure."

Jennifer understood well enough what Samson had in mind, though it made her rather nervous to think that someone might be listening to every word they said. "Yes, that sounds like fun," she answered. "Would you be my guide, Samson?"

"Willingly. But we must ask permission of the Lord Chancellor, and he may not readily grant it. The safety of the Royal Family is in his charge, you know. You are an important person now, Jennifer, and such people may not always go where they please."

"Oh." Jennifer had hoped to have nothing more to do with Rinaldo if she could help it, but it seemed there was no avoiding him. "How do I go about asking his permission?" she asked. "I may not be seeing him again for days, for all I know."

Samson chuckled. "You forget you are a princess," he continued in a low voice. "Rinaldo is your servant, at least in theory, as is every man, woman and child in Eladeria save only the King himself. If you send to summon him he cannot refuse. He may not like it, but he will come."

"Of course, how stupid of me!" she exclaimed. "But who should take the message, Samson? You?"

"I think not," said the dwarf with a twisted smile. "I am but a jester and not worthy to be a princess's messenger, you know." He crossed to the outer door of the chamber and opened it. "Herald!" he called. "The Princess commands you!"

At once a young man in the colourful livery of a herald appeared. He had apparently been standing in the corridor all the while in case Jennifer needed him. It also seemed that he had been napping at his post, for his eyes were sleepy and only half open.

"Your Highness?"

"Herald, bear a message to the Lord High Chancellor, if you please. Tell Duke Rinaldo that I request the pleasure of his company at his earliest convenience."

"Yes, Highness. Here in your chamber?"

"That's right. No, wait a minute. Not here. In the Great Hall, herald. Tell the Duke that I will be expecting him in the Great Hall in ten minutes."

"Highness."

The herald turned to go but Jennifer called him back.

"One more thing, herald. Go also to the Lord High Steward and tell him that the Princess will be ready for her supper in an hour's time. Tell him I want nothing fancy, but I would be grateful for a dish of ice cream for dessert. Chocolate, if possible. And something for my jester as well. Can you remember all that, herald?"

"Yes, your Highness."

The young man left at a run. Jennifer laughed.

"That was fun!" she said. "Every girl should be a princess."

"If that were so," objected Samson, "who would be left to serve you?"

"The boys!" Jennifer replied. "Who else?"

Samson chuckled. Then he said, "Summoning Rinaldo to the Great Hall was a good idea, Jennifer. An excellent idea. He will hardly be able to refuse your request in front of the whole court."

"Let's hope not," Jennifer answered. "I don't think he's going to be very happy about it though. Anyway, we'd better get going. I don't think it would help matters to keep him waiting."

With Samson at her side she entered the Great Hall and strode up to Rinaldo. With the whole court looking on as he considered Jennifer's request, there was nothing he could do but allow her and Samson to make their planned expedition.

"It shall be as your Highness commands," he told her, speaking more respectfully than usual for the benefit of the heralds and guards standing nearby. "However, it would be dangerous for your Highness to go out into the city with only the Fool"—here he indicated Samson—"to attend you. No, your Highness shall go disguised and well guarded. I shall appoint two or three of my personal bodyguards to escort you."

"Thank you, Rinaldo," Jennifer replied in a calm voice. "You are most thoughtful. Please instruct your men to be ready first thing in the morning. You may go now."

Inwardly, though, her heart was sinking. It would be impossible to hold private conversation with Samson with Rinaldo's guards hovering nearby. Trust Rinaldo to think of everything! However, there was nothing she could do but accept his offer.

Supper was another huge meal, with more chocolate ice cream than she and Samson could possibly eat and a note from Duke Hugo apologizing for not being able to serve it himself.

Later, in the middle of a game of chess that Samson was winning handily, Dame Isobel came to help Jennifer prepare for bed. The old woman asked no questions about the events of the day, but once or twice Jennifer caught her making sidelong glances at her that seemed to say: Poor child! If only she knew!

Jennifer, though, was comfortable in the knowledge that the worst that could happen to her was that she would wake up in her own world—though that would be bad enough, she thought. She fell sound asleep as soon as her head touched the pillow.

6

Attack from above

The next day dawned bright and clear, with the banners on the palace rooftops fluttering gently in a warm breeze from the south. After a breakfast that seemed to go on forever, Jennifer, Samson and three of Rinaldo's guards met at the palace doors.

All five were dressed in the fashion of the town, which was almost as colourful but much simpler than that of the palace. Samson seemed especially pleased to be out of his foolish jester's costume for the day. Jennifer thought he looked much better for the change, even though his small size and long beard made a real disguise impossible.

Jennifer herself had been given a simple pale yellow tunic by Dame Isobel, and a pair of stout leather shoes much the same as she might have worn for a day's walk in what she still thought of as the real world.

Rinaldo met them at the palace gate and warned them to be back at the palace by sunset. "Otherwise I shall have to assume that you have been kidnapped," he explained. "Above all, do not say or do anything that might reveal who you really are."

Jennifer nodded and bade the Chancellor good-bye, and the party set off at once. The guards did not smile or talk, even amongst themselves, but marched along together in a small group a few paces behind Jennifer and Samson. Jennifer knew that the guards were staying just close enough to hear everything she and the jester said.

Their presence made it impossible to follow Samson's original plan, which had, of course, been to find a quiet spot where they could sit and exchange information with no fear of being spied upon. Jennifer decided that she would just have to play at being a tourist and keep her eyes open for any opportunity to escape the watchfulness of the guards.

Unfortunately this proved impossible. Their way took them to the main square of Tumbol, where the greatest merchants had their shops and where the crowds were thickest.

If Jennifer had had less on her mind she could have wished for nothing better than to browse among the huge tables full of strange goods that surrounded them everywhere they went. There were shops that dealt in scrolls with bright pictures painted on them by hand. There were others where goldsmiths and silversmiths sold such jewellery as even a princess might wish for. Still other shops sold weapons—grim-looking swords with jewelled hilts, pikes, crossbows and great spiked clubs.

There were clothing shops of every kind, of course, and in some of these Jennifer bought a few things with gold coins from a purse given her by

Rinaldo. She made the guards carry her purchases, hoping that these burdens might slow the men down enough that she could exchange a few private words with Samson, but they followed as closely as ever.

Even where the crowds were thickest the guards somehow managed to stay close at all times. Finally, when Jennifer felt she could walk no longer, she suggested that they stop for lunch. Samson quickly found them an inn with a large empty table in the corner.

The jester apparently had some idea of making the guards too drunk to carry out their orders, for he continually offered them wine, but the men would not drink. Neither did they eat, except that one of them would taste every dish brought to Jennifer, for fear that it was poisoned.

When the meal was over and the landlord had been paid, they went again into the square. Jennifer felt she could not bear to spend the afternoon shopping, so she suggested that they find a place where they could sit down for a while until the worst heat of the day was over, for by now the sun was shining fiercely.

Samson had just begun to lead them across the square to a park he knew of when suddenly someone in the great crowd of people cried out in a terrified voice that carried above the bustle, "The sky! In the sky! Look to your lives!"

The shouting was taken up at once by other voices. Everywhere people were standing frozen, pointing up into the sky, or else running headlong as if in fear for their lives. The guards looked no less alarmed than anyone else. They appeared to be torn between protecting their Princess from danger and fleeing themselves.

Samson clutched Jennifer's arm and pointed into the eastern sky. At last Jennifer saw what was causing the panic.

There were six of them, great yellow creatures flying swiftly, more swiftly than any bird, and as they flew they uttered a weird piercing cry that made Jennifer's blood run cold. They were three times the size of eagles, she guessed, though they were still too far away for her to be sure.

As they drew nearer Jennifer could make them out more clearly. The hot sun glinted on their powerful wings as though their feathers were of brass, and their wingtips as well as their legs had huge claws like curved daggers.

Their faces were most horrible of all. They had no feathers, but were in the shape of human faces—girls' faces—with small eyes, fangs like razors that protruded over their thin lips and hair like spun brass streaming behind them.

"Harpies!" yelled Samson above the uproar. "Creatures of Swenhild! Run for your life!"

Just then a knot of terrified townspeople pushed by in front of the guards before the latter could stop them.

"Now!" hissed Samson in Jennifer's ear. "Take my hand!"

They plunged together into the crowd, leaving the bewildered guards behind them. People were running in every direction, trying to get indoors before the harpies were upon them. Glancing back as she ran, Jennifer caught a last glimpse of one of the guards searching desperately in the confused mass of people for some sign of herself and Samson. Good riddance! she thought, and kept running.

With Samson guiding them they somehow fought their way across the square, the journey becoming gradually easier as the crowd cleared. Then they ducked down a narrow lane between two shops and picked their way through the litter until they came to a small door.

Samson knocked three times. A moment later the door was answered by a bald, ancient man, all bones and skin, with half-moon spectacles perched on the tip of his nose and a tuft of beard on his chin.

"Samson, my good friend!" he cried in a stronger voice than one would have expected. "Come in, come in! This is an unexpected pleasure! What brings you here on a fine midsummer day? Why aren't you lolling about the palace grounds as usual, taking the sun?"

"Prospero, you old muddlebrain," returned the dwarf, "we are here for our safety. Haven't you heard the commotion? Harpies are coming, man, half a dozen of them! Quick, let us go upstairs to the window!"

"Of course I heard," said Prospero calmly. "I'm not deaf, despite my years. Well, not *too* deaf. But you needn't have worried about the harpies, my dear fellow. They won't be taking anyone today. No, this is just *her* way of warning the town, that's all. Just a reminder a few days before the Tribute so that nothing should go amiss when the time comes."

As he finished speaking Prospero looked closely at Jennifer for the first time and his manner became suddenly grave.

"Yes, the Tribute!" he said musingly. "Golden hair, blue eyes. What are you up to, Samson? Do come upstairs, and hurry. You too, my dear. Yes, you had better see this."

With no more explanation he led them up a narrow staircase into a tiny, musty room crammed from floor to ceiling with scrolls and strange apparatus. Jennifer, who had understood little of the old man's conversation with Samson, followed her two companions to the window and looked on in amazement at the scene unfolding outside.

The harpies were just over the rooftops. Now that she had a better chance to look at them Jennifer saw that she had not been far wrong in her guess at their size. Their girl-faces writhed in expressions of pain and hate and their shrill cries, now deafeningly loud, lanced her soul like slivers of icy terror.

They were wheeling around the square, now darting high to clear an overhanging roof, now swooping downward till their outstretched talons almost raked the ground. At times they came so near the window at which Jennifer was standing that their clawed wingtips almost scratched against the pane and then she could see their eyes, frosty blue and pitiless, and their befanged mouths, twisted with cruelty and spite.

Some of the braver citizens, men and women both, let fly with arrows from the windows, but with no effect. For, as Jennifer now saw, the harpies' feathers were indeed made of brass or some like metal; the shafts bounced harmlessly off them onto the ground below.

This awful spectacle continued for almost a quarter of an hour. Then, with a final chorus of ear-splitting shrieks, the monstrous creatures climbed back into the skies on their broad wings and departed into the east whence they had come.

At last Jennifer could turn away from the window, unclench her knotted fists and draw a decent breath again. She was not surprised to discover that she was shaking; even her two companions were pale.

Prospero rummaged in a corner of the room until he found some chairs. He looked thoughtfully at Jennifer for a long while before he said, "You did well, my dear. Very well. I have watched strong men faint dead away at the sight you have just seen. But now will you have some tea, both of you? And then I think we will want to talk. Is that not so?"

7
Prospero

By the time Propsero returned a few moments later with a tray of tea and cookies, Jennifer had almost recovered her calm. Now she faced her companions eagerly, hoping at last for some answers to the questions that had been forming in her mind.

"Well, Samson," Prospero began, "perhaps it would be well if you were to introduce me to your friend."

"Of course," the jester said. "Prospero, I would like you to meet her Royal Highness, the Princess Miranda, known in her own world as Jennifer. And Jennifer, this is my old friend Prospero, seller of scrolls, scholar, and master of wizardry."

Prospero rose to bow, then sat back down with a chuckle.

"Samson does me too much honour," he told Jennifer. "Seller of scrolls I certainly am, and perhaps in my own small way a scholar. But alas, I am no master of wizardry! A handful of simple spells, a healing charm or two—that is the whole of my skill. But come, there are more important matters to discuss."

This was what Jennifer had been waiting for.

"Yes. Please tell me what all this is about. Samson has given me hints, bits and pieces, but no more. What's this nonsense about me being a princess, to start with? We all know that I'm no princess. Rinaldo knows it, you and Samson both know it. Why, I think everybody knows it! So why is everyone pretending? And what's this Tribute you were talking about just now? Does that have something to do with me? And those harpies! What are they and who sent them? And how did I get *into* this crazy world anyway?" Jennifer had to pause to catch her breath.

"Well, that last one's easy enough," said Samson with a smile. "You fell asleep and you're dreaming. At least that's what you told me. Don't you remember?"

"Yes, that's right, I'd forgotten," Jennifer admitted uncomfortably. "I did tell you that, didn't I?" Somehow it seemed rather impolite to tell people you liked that they were only characters in your dream. "But that isn't what I meant just now. I want to know how *you* think I got here."

Samson made no reply.

"Dreaming," mused Prospero. "Yes, that makes sense. Of course you would think that; it's only natural. Who knows, it may even be true, although I must say it doesn't feel that way to me. But then, I may be dreaming myself. How can one tell?"

Jennifer found this too confusing to think about.

"Let's forget about dreams for a minute," she begged. "I want to know—"

"How you came to Eladeria," finished Prospero. "Yes, of course you do. Well, that's very simple and very complicated at the same time. The simple answer is that you were brought here by magic from another world—*your* world. The spell is a very powerful and ancient one; in all the Kingdom only Duke Rinaldo knows it. Where he learned it none know, though I can guess easily enough. For now, I need only say that every year for the past seven years a driverless carriage-and-four has arrived in Tumbol on Midsummer Day, bearing in it a golden-haired maiden with blue eyes to be our Princess. The seventh time it bore you."

"The seventh time!" exclaimed Jennifer. "So that's what King Theobald meant. Wait though—that doesn't make any sense. If I'm the seventh where are the other six? Why doesn't anyone ever mention them? Have you ever seen them?"

"I have," Prospero replied slowly, his voice suddenly older. "I saw them only today. So did you, Jennifer."

There was an awful silence.

"The harpies!" breathed Jennifer at last. "They became the harpies!"

Sudden fear clutched at her throat and for a moment all she wanted to do was leap from her seat and run, away from her two friends, away from Eladeria, away from everything. But her knees were jelly and she knew she could not so much as stand, let alone run.

Now was the time to wake herself up, she thought

suddenly. Now, before anything dreadful happened. But a curious feeling deep inside her kept her from trying, a feeling of anger towards Rinaldo and whoever was in league with him, mingled with a desire to see him punished and his victims set free. Gradually the fear left her, but the anger still burned hot in her blue eyes.

"How?" she demanded at last. "Why? Tell me."

"As you may have guessed," replied Prospero, "the answer to that lies in the east. There, in a great castle all of black stone, between a high cliff and a jungle of thorny trees, dwells Swenhild, the greatest sorceress of her age—and the wickedest."

"The old hag?" asked Jennifer. "The one the King mentioned?"

"The same," said Samson grimly. "It is she who sends the harpies, and it is she who made them."

"That is so," Prospero agreed. "They are her eyes and ears in the wide world, and they are her hands to reach out and take what she wants. If she craves gold, the harpies will bring it. If it is jewels she wants, or other treasure, it is the harpies she sends to find it. And if she needs a human being for one of her foul spells, the harpies will bring her one. She rules their minds, Jennifer, and their souls. They know it and hate her for it, but they are powerless to disobey her."

"But how does she do it?" asked Jennifer, her voice quivering with horror. "I mean, how does she—make them?"

"That is known only to her," answered the old man. "But it must be a potent spell indeed that needs a princess for its working. Who knows how she came upon it or how she lured the true Princess, Princess Julia, the King's own daughter, to be her first victim? Yet that is what she did."

"The *true* Princess!" Jennifer exclaimed. "One who wasn't adopted? That makes me really the eighth then. But didn't the King try to save her?"

"He did," said Prospero, "but it only brought him further sorrow. He himself could not be spared, you see, from matters of state that pressed heavily upon him at the time. So instead of going himself he sent Prince Corbold, his only son, to find Julia and bring her home if he could."

"Prince Corbold! Samson told me he disappeared on a hunting expedition."

"So it was called by the King," Prospero explained, "in order that the people should not know that an evil sorceress dwelt almost on their doorstep. It is true, though, that he vanished, and there is little doubt that Swenhild was behind it, though whether she killed him or did some other evil to him none know. Perhaps Samson could say more of these things than I can, however, for he came out of the east not long after."

"No," said Samson, looking quite ill at ease. "Such things are beyond me, Prospero. I know nothing of them."

After a little pause Prospero continued. "However that may be, Princess Julia became the first and mightiest of the harpies. She does not fly with the other six, which is why she was not among them today. No, Swenhild saves her for other duties, those that she will trust to no other. It is she, for example, who comes to bear away the Tribute."

"Yes, the Tribute. Explain that to me," said Jennifer.

Prospero looked at her hard before answering, as if he were trying to see in her face whether she had the courage to hear his reply. But when he spoke his voice was firm and unhesitating.

"The Tribute is the price Swenhild demands for leaving our land in peace," he began. "It is the greatest of her crimes, and Eladeria's greatest shame. Each year, as we have told you, Rinaldo's sorcery summons a maiden from your world to ours. By a Proclamation of Adoption she is made a princess, and is treated as one; but alas, not for long.

"On the night of the full moon next after Midsummer Day she is given a drink of mead and soothing herbs to make her sleep, then taken to a hill near the palace. All the palace household, commoners and nobles both, stand around her in a wide circle. They are dressed in white robes so that in the full moon's light the circle is easily seen from the air. At midnight the harpy comes to carry her off into the east. You know now what comes after."

"Yes, I know," said Jennifer. Anger was beginning to rise in her again. "What I *don't* know is why! Why do the people let it happen? Why don't they stop this dreadful thing? Are they so afraid?"

"In part, yes," answered Prospero sadly. "They *are* afraid, and with reason. You saw Swenhild's creatures a while ago and were afraid yourself. Who would not be? And that was just a warning. Had they been intent on real mischief the harpies would have come in under cover of cloud, or flying low, to escape being seen until it was too late. You saw their claws, their speed, their strength. Many would fall under such an attack, which would surely come if the Tribute were not paid. Yes, there is reason for fear.

"Then there is Rinaldo. For years I have guessed that he is in league with her, and I no longer have any doubt. What she has promised him in return I do not know—the Kingdom itself probably. It is he who holds the others back when they talk of resisting her, saying that the lives of the princesses are a small price to pay to avoid Swenhild's revenge. With him, though, it is not fear but his own ambitious greed that bends him to the service of the witch. The townsfolk, I am sure, would find their courage soon enough were it not for him. He is the greatest reason why the Tribute still goes on."

"He is the greatest reason for a lot of things," exclaimed Jennifer. "The King's illness, for one. I'm almost sure Rinaldo uses some kind of magic to control the King. Is that possible?"

"Very much so," Prospero replied. "Those who love the King have long suspected it. But how did you discover this?"

"It was yesterday," Jennifer told him, "when I went to see the King. Rinaldo seemed to be able to turn him on and off like a—like a lightbulb."

"I know not what this 'lightbulb' that you speak of may be," said Prospero, "but I'm sure that you are right."

"Yes," Samson put in. "But did you not tell me, Jennifer, that the King had whispered something to you alone? That for a moment he had escaped control? What was it? What did my—the King say?"

"Let me see," Jennifer said. "It was when I went over to his bed and kissed him. Rinaldo didn't like *that,* by the way."

"It was well done," Prospero assured her. "It may have been that and nothing more that gave his Majesty the strength to speak. A kiss may be stronger than a spell, sometimes."

"Anyway," Jennifer went on, "he grabbed me suddenly and whispered in my ear. If I heard him right, his exact words were 'The Paladian Scroll, child! Find it! Use it! Your only chance!'"

8
The Stone of Seeking

At Jennifer's words Samson started and Prospero nearly jumped out of his chair.

"What? What did you say? The Paladian Scroll?"

"That's what he called it," Jennifer replied, puzzled by their obvious surprise. "Then he said, 'Beware Rinaldo! Beware him!' Is the Scroll that important?"

"Important?" replied Prospero. "Yes, it is very important. At least it may be. But tell me, did Rinaldo hear this?"

"No, I don't think so. He saw the King whispering to me and when we left he asked me about it. I told him the King said 'Bless you, my child' and something else that I hadn't heard properly. He laughed at that, but I think he believed me."

Samson chuckled. "Well done!" he exclaimed. "That's one up on my Lord the Duke!"

"Well done, indeed," agreed Prospero. "If Rinaldo knew or suspected that the Paladian Scroll really existed and was not just a myth-maker's fancy he would not rest until he held it in his hands. And then he would be powerful beyond measure, and beyond any hope of ours to undo him."

Jennifer's eyes widened. "Why?" she wanted to know. "What is the Paladian Scroll?"

"Alas," Prospero said, "no one knows exactly what it is, except that it is a scroll and that it bears a spell more powerful than any other that has been made. It was devised in an age long ago by Pala, the greatest sorceress that ever lived, to be used by the King or Queen of Eladeria if ever the Kingdom were in such danger that no other help would serve. For long years it was guarded as a great treasure, only to be lost somehow in the Dark Age of Eladeria when the line of the old Royal House was broken. Some believe that it was destroyed in those terrible times; others say that it never existed at all. Until now I myself believed this. But Theobald was always wise in many things and knew much that was hidden from others. These words of his give me hope that the Scroll exists and may be found."

"Found? But how?" cried Samson. "It could be anywhere, if it really does exist, and there is little time. The moon will be full in three days. Eladeria is wide, Prospero—we could not search it all in a lifetime!"

"That is true," replied the old man. "Yet there is hope. It may be that King Theobald had some inkling where the Scroll might be and thought it could be found in time. And, my friends, there is something else."

Prospero rose and crossed the room. He rummaged about among the piles of scrolls and oddments until he came upon a small wooden box with a curved lid, fastened with a silver clasp at the front. He returned to his chair and opened the box for Jennifer and Samson to see.

It held a jewel, clear as any diamond but much larger, almost the size of a grape. The jewel, which was mounted on a slender golden chain, had been cut so that each of its many faces had five equal sides, but it did not sparkle.

"This is a Stone of Seeking," Prospero told them. "It is my greatest treasure. It and two like it were also made by Pala in those long-ago days; few now remember that they exist." He removed the Stone from its box and held it upon his open hand. "When held thus," he went on, "the Stone can lead you to anything that it is in your mind to seek."

"How?" asked Jennifer. "What does it do?"

"It shines," answered the old man. "Look."

At once the Stone began to glow with a brilliant radiance, white and pure, so bright that it drove all shadows from the dimly lit room. Jennifer could hardly bear to look at it.

"I am thinking of you," smiled Prospero, "and it tells me you are near."

Now the jewel dimmed so that its light was like that of a candle seen far away on a dark night: pale, small and flickering.

"I am thinking of Swenhild," said the old man. "She is far away."

And now the Stone of Seeking began to glow more brightly again, though not so much as it had at first. Its light was strong and unwavering, like that of the full moon on a clear night. Seeing it,

Prospero gasped and let the Stone fall clattering to the floor.

"What is it?" cried Samson, leaping to his feet. "What's wrong?"

But Jennifer sat still.

"You were thinking about *it,* weren't you?" she asked. "You were thinking about the Paladian Scroll."

Prospero nodded. "I had little hope," the old man muttered. "You see, I attempted this before, six years ago, when first I learned what horrors Swenhild was practising. I had it in my mind to resist her if I could, yet I knew that without some such power as the Paladian Scroll any effort of my poor skill was doomed to fail against such as she. But the Stone, when I tried it, remained dark, and I could do nothing. I did not guess then that Pala had fashioned the Stone to be an instrument of wisdom as well as strength—that it would not aid in the finding of so great a treasure as the Scroll until the time was ripe, until the opportunity for success was at its height. I think that time has come now. I think that the power of the Paladian Scroll was destined not for me, Jennifer, but for you. The Scroll does exist and it is near. *You* must find it!"

He held out the Stone of Seeking to Jennifer, then changed his mind and gave it instead to Samson.

"It will be safer with you, old friend," he said. "There is no telling but that Jennifer's chambers may be searched, and if Rinaldo found that she had the Stone he would know well that something was amiss. Whereas you—"

"Whereas I am beneath Rinaldo's contempt," chuckled Samson wryly, "and thus beneath his notice. I know it well. Why else would he allow me to visit the Princesses year after year as I have done, until at last I found one—you, Jennifer—who was not so bewildered at being in our world or so fearful of Rinaldo's anger that she could not aid us in the battle against Swenhild? Why else would Rinaldo allow me to accompany you into town today, knowing I would do anything to see him crushed, unless he thought me too small and foolish to harm him? You are right, Prospero, I—"

He was interrupted by a commotion from the street, the sound of a door banging and an exchange of angry voices. Jennifer rushed to the window and looked down.

"The guards!" she told the others. "They must have been looking for us all this time. Now they're getting close."

"Well, well," said Samson calmly. "Then I suggest that we should find them before they find us."

Prospero nodded. "That would be best," he agreed as he led them back to the stairway. "Though there is much more I should like to discuss with you. I should like also to hear of your world, Jennifer. Ah, well. Another time, we must hope. Now go, and may fortune be with you. Farewell, my good friends. Be careful!"

They thanked him and hastened downstairs and into the little lane. Samson led Jennifer around behind some buildings to the other side of the square, not wishing the guards to make any connection between their reappearance and Prospero's rooms. Then they strolled across the square as though nothing at all had happened, coming up behind the three guards just as they were about to knock at another door. The men did not hear the two friends approaching.

"So there you are!" Jennifer exclaimed. "We've been looking all over for you!"

The guards nearly jumped out of their skins.

"Y-your Highness!" one of them stammered. "W-where has your Highness been?"

"Where have *I* been?" retorted Jennifer. "Where have *you* been? Running away from us like that! Anything could have happened to me and who would have prevented it? A fine lot of guards you are!"

"We did not run away, your Highness!" the man protested. "When the harpies came—"

"Yet that is what I shall have to tell Duke Rinaldo," Jennifer interrupted, "if he asks why you were not with me."

The three guards looked terrified. They had no doubt experienced Rinaldo's anger before.

"Of course," Jennifer went on smoothly, "we needn't tell the Duke."

"I beg your Highness, do not tell him."

"Very well," she said after a moment. "This time nothing shall be said. Only see that you are not so careless in the future."

"Your Highness is most kind. Thank you, your Highness!"

"And now," Jennifer announced, "it is time that we were returning."

So saying, she took Samson's arm and set off. The dwarf was still grinning at the guards' discomfiture when they arrived back at the palace.

9
Prisoner!

Jennifer tossed and turned in bed that night, unable to fall asleep. She had not seen Samson since their return to the palace. She had been expecting that he would join her for supper but he had not. Now she was very worried that something had happened to him.

What if Rinaldo had discovered that the jester had the Stone of Seeking? It was even possible that the Chancellor's spies had overheard the meeting with Prospero that afternoon. If that were true, Rinaldo would undoubtedly find some means of getting Samson out of the way, knowing that without the dwarf's aid Jennifer would be helpless.

The dreadful thought even crossed Jennifer's mind that Prospero himself was in league with Rinaldo. She had liked the old man and trusted him at once, but now, alone in the stillness of her dark chamber, fears that she would have laughed away in the clear light of day were not so easily put aside.

Outside, the palace bells were tolling midnight.

With the passing of a cloud the light of the waxing moon burst in through the window, making weird shadows in the room. The gloomy peal of the deep-voiced bells faded at last into a silence that was broken only by the creaking of the walls and the chirrupping of insects on the lawn.

Then suddenly Jennifer sat bolt upright in her bed, her heart thumping wildly. In the shadows that lined the walls of the chamber something had moved, and even with her heartbeat pounding in her ears she could hear the sound of quiet breathing. She was not alone!

There was another movement in the dark, and then a section of the wall suddenly swung out into the room. A cloaked and hooded figure came out of the shadows and made straight for her. She gasped, but with relief, for the intruder was no taller than herself.

"Samson!" she exclaimed softly. "Oh, I'm so glad it's you! I was afraid you were Rinaldo coming to take me away! But where have you been? And what are you doing here now?"

"Quick, get up and put your clothes on," the dwarf replied abruptly. "We have work to do."

Jennifer rose immediately and began to get dressed. When she was ready Samson reached inside his cloak and pulled out the Stone of Seeking. He concentrated for a moment and the Stone began to glow brilliantly, lighting the whole room with its clear white light. An instant later it dimmed again and Samson put it away.

"The Paladian Scroll!" he whispered. "It's right here in the palace! I checked with the Stone as soon as I was by myself this evening and I've been tracking it ever since. I know where it is, Jennifer! Now we must get it!"

Jennifer's face lit up with sudden hope. "Show me the way!" she said excitedly. "Let's not waste any time!"

Samson nodded and took her hand. "Through here," he said. "Back into the wall."

They passed together through the low gap where the wall had swung open and into a low and narrow passage, its stone floor thick with the dust of many years. Samson pulled on a handle set into the wall and the panel swung shut again, leaving the pair in utter darkness.

"How do we find our way?" asked Jennifer nervously. "I can't see a thing."

"Don't worry," he reassured her. A moment later the strong, clear light of the Stone of Seeking burst out from the palm of his hand.

Now Jennifer could see that the passage sloped sharply downward from where they stood. The walls were rough, dark green and slippery with moss. The ceiling loomed only a hand's-breadth above Jennifer's head.

"For once I am glad of my height!" said Samson. "These passages run the whole length and breadth of the palace, but they were not built for comfort. They were made long ago for the use of the Royal Family in times of danger. Few know of them; I doubt that even Rinaldo realizes they exist."

The light of the Stone had vanished as Samson spoke. Now he renewed his concentration and the

Stone sprang back to life. He held it out before him, pointing the way.

"Right," said Jennifer. "Let's go."

The passage curved and twisted so much that Jennifer soon lost all sense of direction. Frequently they came to forks, but since Samson knew where he was going these were not a problem. The light of the Stone of Seeking grew steadily stronger until at last it was so brilliant that Jennifer knew they must be nearing their destination.

Abruptly Samson stopped. There was a brass handle set into the wall here, a twin of the one outside Jennifer's bedchamber. Samson allowed the light of the Stone to go out and at the same time grasped the handle and pulled. The wall opened to reveal, when their eyes had adjusted to the dim light that trickled in through a small, high window, a large chamber lined with shelf upon shelf of dusty scrolls and heavy books. By the thin moonlight the room had an eerie look that made Jennifer shudder.

"What is this place?" she whispered. "Where are we?"

"It is Rinaldo's library," Samson whispered back. "That door over there opens onto a corridor. The one on the other side leads into his bedchamber. We must be very quiet if we are not to disturb him—he is not a heavy sleeper."

They advanced into the room and the wall swung shut behind them, leaving no crack. Samson pointed to a tiny mark on the stone wall, a hollow like the wrinkle on a pea.

"To open the wall you must push here," he explained. "Do not forget. There is a spring, so the wall will close on its own when you have passed through. Now, to find the Scroll."

It was not easy. With the Stone of Seeking cupped in his hands to make sure that its light did not escape through the crack under the door to Rinaldo's bedchamber, Samson walked up and down the long shelves, watching closely for any slight change in the Stone's radiance. It reminded Jennifer of the game of Hunt the Thimble she had sometimes played at parties.

"Now he's getting warmer," she thought as she followed her friend in and out among the shelves. "No, cooler again. Still cooler. Very cold now. Ah, that's better! Warmer, warmer. Now he's getting hot! No, not that way—cooler again. Yes, to the left, that's it! Hotter, very hot! Absolutely boiling now!"

"I've found it," whispered Samson, and the Stone of Seeking went out.

In his hand Samson held an ancient yellow scroll, its edges blackened with age. It was rolled up tightly and bound with a short length of gold wire.

"It was on the bottom shelf," Samson said, "behind a lot of old history books. Goodness knows how many centuries it has lain there! Quick now, take it, open it! See what it says!"

Jennifer's hands were trembling as she struggled to remove the gold wire. What strange mysteries would the ancient Scroll reveal? How would she use it?

The wire came loose at last and Samson took it from her and put it in his pocket. In the dim light she unrolled the Scroll very gently, afraid that it might be dry and brittle and crumble in her hands. But when it was fully open she gave a sigh of disappointment.

"We've got the wrong one somehow." she told Samson. "This one isn't a spell, just a—a picture of something."

Actually it was a design, a curious and complicated web of coloured lines that seemed to glow with a light of their own. Jennifer stared at it raptly for some seconds, strangely unable to remove her gaze from the parchment. Whether by some property of the design itself or merely by a trick of the light, the coloured lines seemed to bend and flow as she stared, yet the pattern itself did not change.

Finally she tore her eyes away from the scroll and said, "Well, what do we do now? Keep looking?"

No sooner were the words out of her mouth, though, than there was a puff of smoke and the Scroll turned instantly to dust in her hands. Not a trace of it remained. Jennifer let out a squeal of alarm as she found herself suddenly holding onto empty air, and at once there came an angry cry from the next room as Rinaldo awoke.

"Quick!" hissed Samson. "Into the passage!"

He tore across the room and thumbed the hidden latch, with Jennifer close behind him. But her cloak caught on a nail sticking out from one of the shelves and she fell down just as Samson was disappearing into the wall. Before she could regain her feet the door to Rinaldo's bedchamber flew open and the Chancellor himself stormed in, dressed in a purple nightrobe and slippers.

"What is the meaning of this?" he roared. "What

are you doing here?" He advanced on her threateningly. "Answer me, little fool!"

"I-I-I was just looking for you, Rinaldo," Jennifer stammered, seeking desperately for some story that the furious man would believe. "I heard noises outside my chamber and I was afraid, so I was coming to you for help!"

"Nonsense!" growled Rinaldo. "Do you take me for a simpleton? With guards outside your chamber you would hardly be likely to come to *me* for help. I do not know what brings you snooping about in here, little fool, but I will see that you do it no more."

Now Rinaldo waved his arms in a strange manner and muttered a few words under his breath. Then he went to the door and shouted for a guard. When a man appeared a moment later, Rinaldo faced him furiously.

"How did the Princess get in here without my knowing, you nincompoop? Why didn't you stop her? You must have been sleeping on your feet!"

"B-b-but Lord—"

"Enough! Save your excuses! Listen carefully. The Princess is not well in her mind—just a moment ago I found her wandering in here not knowing where she was or what she was doing. I have placed her under a Spell of Tranquillity for her own protection; she is clearly overwrought. Take her up to her chamber now and see that she remains there. From now on she must have no visitors and she must not leave her room. See that a guard is with her in her bedchamber at all times."

When he had finished rattling off these orders Rinaldo turned to go back to bed. But before he left he growled, "As for your incompetence, guard, be sure that it will be dealt with later!"

10
The Tribute

Jennifer watched despairingly as Rinaldo went away. The fleeting thought crossed her mind that she could rush across the room to the wall and escape into the hidden passage before the guard could stop her. But it was too late for that. Even supposing she could find her way through the passages, which was far from certain, Rinaldo now had an excuse for locking her up in her chambers and he would spare no effort until she was found again.

Besides, she thought glumly, Rinaldo would know that I must have had help to find the passages, and that would mean trouble for Samson.

So when the guard said, "If you will please come with me, your Highness?" Jennifer had no choice but to obey.

As they walked through the corridors, empty at this hour except for a few unblinking guards, she wondered what Rinaldo had meant by saying that he had put her under a Spell of Tranquillity. It was hard to be sure just what such a spell might do, but

Jennifer supposed that it was meant to make her drowsy or dazed, and less likely to give trouble.

Well, that's one of Rinaldo's plans that didn't come off, anyway, she told herself. If he thinks I feel even a little bit tranquil he's sadly mistaken. Mad as a hornet would be more like it! Still, there's no point in letting *him* know his spell didn't work.

Keeping this in mind, Jennifer did not speak or so much as turn her head all the way back to her quarters, and once or twice she even feigned a stumble, as though she could hardly stay awake. Then they were there and her escort put her in the care of the door-guard, passing on Rinaldo's instructions that she be strictly confined to her bedchamber.

"Be gentle with her, Benio," he said before he left to return to his post. "The Duke has put a Spell of Tranquillity on her and the poor lass can barely stand up. But remember, no visitors or Rinaldo will have both our hides!"

Benio nodded and led Jennifer back to her bed. With no choice now but to keep up her pretence of being under a spell, Jennifer crawled under the covers and lay still. But it was a long time before she could sleep.

The next three days were the longest and dreariest she had ever spent. Being locked up in her room was bad enough, but having no one to talk things over with was ten times worse. The stolid guards neither said nor did anything that hinted at how Samson was faring or what Rinaldo was up to. Day and night the men took their turns just inside her door, never stirring except to change shifts or to bring Jennifer her meals. The rush of defiance she had felt when Rinaldo had cast his Spell of Tranquillity gradually evaporated. By degrees her anger wore itself down to a dull resentment, and her eagerness to thwart Rinaldo gave way to weary astonishment that she had been so foolish as to even make the attempt.

On the second day Jennifer overheard Benio worriedly telling one of his fellows that Rinaldo had expected her to recover from the Spell of Tranquillity in no more than twelve hours. Now she could at last give up her act of being always sleepy and confused; in that there was some relief. It did nothing to change her situation, though, apart from giving her the freedom to stretch her legs by pacing.

With her breakfast the next morning she received news of a sort. As she bit into a muffin her teeth closed on something hard and leathery that proved to be a tightly rolled slip of parchment. After glancing at the guard to check that he wasn't watching, Jennifer unrolled it and read: *Saw P. in town today. Don't lose hope. S.*

Good old Samson! So he hadn't forgotten her. Yes, going to Prospero for advice was just the thing to do. For the first time in days Jennifer had something to be cheerful about. Yet now she fretted more than ever.

Don't lose hope. Was Samson just trying to be comforting or did he really believe they could still win? Jennifer could not imagine how. It seemed that the Paladian Scroll, wherever it was, was going to be of no help after all, and the full moon would rise that very night. The chances seemed slim that Samson could manage her rescue before the Tribute.

There was nothing to do, though, but wait. And now that the horror of the approaching Tribute drew nearer, the hours did not drag out as they had, but passed more and more swiftly. It was as though time itself were a party to Rinaldo's plans and galloped where it had once crawled. Jennifer waited for her rescue with mounting anxiety, but still it did not come.

The sun did not set majestically that evening; rather, it plummeted impatiently past the horizon as though fearful of lingering to mar the splendour of the full moon. Black night descended on the palace like a cloud of ink. One by one the stars appeared. The solemn, questioning cries of the awakening owls filled the still air like echoes of tormented souls howling for peace. Now a ray of silver appeared, a cold needle of light over the distant hills, and the swollen moon arose to take possession of the skies.

Jennifer's hands were trembling now; her breath was unsteady, coming in ragged gasps. She held her hands clenched stiffly at her sides and would not let herself cry, but in her mind was a tight knot of fear that no strength of hers could unravel.

Now is the time to wake myself up, she thought desperately. I can't go through with the Tribute—it would be crazy! Samson and Prospero are just dream people. I don't owe them anything, even if they have been nice to me.

But somehow she could not quite convince herself that it would be fair to desert her friends even now, even when she had no way to be completely sure that they had not deserted her. If this was a dream it was no ordinary one. Could Jennifer *know* that Samson and Prospero had no existence outside her mind?

No, she decided reluctantly. I can't leave them to Swenhild and Rinaldo no matter how bad it gets. I have to do my best to help them first.

It wasn't that she was any less terrified than before, for the terror of dreams is real even if the cause of it is no more than illusion. But now that she had made up her mind to carry on, Jennifer no longer thought of waking herself. Instead she resigned herself to waiting, prepared to act if an opportunity should arise.

Soon the door to the chamber opened and one of Rinaldo's personal guards entered bearing a golden goblet on a tray.

"Drink, your Highness," he said. "This brew will bring you ease."

"I'm not thirsty," Jennifer answered hoarsely. "I don't want it."

"Nevertheless, Highness, it is the Duke's command that you drink it. It would be foolish to disobey."

The guard's tone was respectful, but Jennifer did not mistake the threat behind his words. If she refused to drink, what then? Rinaldo undoubtedly had unpleasant methods of ensuring that she would not refuse twice. She was powerless and she knew it.

Numbly she took the goblet and swallowed the soothing liquid without further resistance. It was honeyed and went down easily. Then she sat down on the edge of her bed with her head between her hands.

The guard had spoken truly. Though its power was that of nature and not of magic, Rinaldo's herb potion was not to be resisted. Before long Jennifer's tense muscles began to relax and a fog of drowsiness stole over her, stilling her fear and muddling her thoughts. She hardly noticed when Rinaldo came in shortly afterwards with six of his men, and she did not protest when he took her arm to lead her away.

She was conducted through the twining palace corridors by a route that brought her to a side door opening onto a broad meadow, less trimly kept than the rest of the grounds. A single tall hill loomed like a grim shadow before her.

Rinaldo halted and they waited on the meadow's edge and watched. Their appearance at the door must have been a signal, for at once a muffled drum began to thud in a slow, steady measure, its hollow tone treading the night like ghostly footsteps.

Doors creaked open here and there along the palace walls. From them people came forth in single file, wrapped from toe to crown in cloaks of white, cowled to conceal their faces. The marchers neither spoke nor turned their heads, but went silently forward to the beat of the ghostly drum, their files gradually merging into one.

The doors clanged shut one by one as the last of the white-clad figures joined the procession. Like a huge white snake the silent throng wound its way across the meadow to the hill. The head of the column coiled around the hill and out of sight, only to reappear a few moments later, completing the ring.

The drum suddenly slowed, expectantly, ominously, but the dull sound of its thudding was less horrifying than the unnatural silence into which each drumbeat died. All was in readiness.

The potion's grip on Jennifer's mind tightened as she was led across the grass. The drum, the night, the silent watchers, all fell away from her drugged mind. The fear was the last to go—it clung to her like a curse when all else was forgotten. But at last the fear too was stilled.

The guards left her, and Rinaldo himself picked her up in his arms and carried her to a flat stone slab at the hillcrest. There he laid her under the full moon's unblinking eye. The drum stopped; dead silence swallowed the night.

For long minutes nothing moved. The white-clad figures stood like so many statues, stock-still in the breathless dark. On the slab Jennifer had closed her eyes to the stars. She slept, alone of all who were there unmindful of her peril.

Then it came, a sound that carried from afar in the heavy air, a wailing cry that froze the heart and strangled hope. Now, too, came a distant beating of metal-feathered pinions that slowly grew to an onward-rushing roar. Like a living spirit of hate the harpy came, saw with her frosted eyes the victim sleeping helplessly below and bent her wings for the pitiless triumph of her descent.

Petrified with sickly fear, the ring of watchers stood and looked on mutely as the harpy's taloned feet opened to clutch her unconscious prey. The claws of brass bit Jennifer's white robe like jaws closing. The harpy Julia threw her cruel head back to set her gaze against the moon, uttering once again her soul-destroying shriek, and still the watchers did not cry out or move.

Except for one.

Even as the harpy gathered her great wings to leap into the skies once more, one small figure broke free of the ring and sprinted up the hill, casting his white robe aside on the grass as he ran. An instant before the harpy had risen beyond his reach he vaulted atop the stone slab, flung himself at a brass-feathered leg and clung there.

The harpy did not waver in her flight, but climbed steadily with her double burden, winging eastward towards Swenhild's lair.

11
Swenhild

Jennifer awoke with cool air streaming past her face and the first rays of the sun lightening the eastern sky to greet her bleary eyes. Below her Eladeria stretched far away to her right; on the left was the endless sea. It was beautiful, so beautiful that it was only after a moment that she became suddenly aware of her desperate position.

In the harpy's powerful grip she hung, helpless to move, trapped beyond hope between the terrifying height and the more terrifying fate that awaited her.

Soon a black shadow arose from the land between her and the rising sun—a tall and jagged cliff at the sea's edge, with a castle at its summit whose jagged towers clawed the pink sky. They were closing fast on Swenhild's foul domain. The harpy's tireless wings seemed to beat ever more strongly as her destination grew nearer.

Oh, Samson! Jennifer wailed in her thoughts. Samson, why couldn't you do anything? Couldn't you even have *tried* to save me?

Bitter tears streamed down her face as she remembered the kindly dwarf who had always seemed so fearless and wise in spite of his small size. It was unfair, so unfair of him to have let this happen to her! She had trusted him!

Then even in the midst of her horror and despair a sudden thought arose to dry her flowing tears. None of this is happening, she told herself. Not really. I'm dreaming. Why do I keep forgetting that? I'm not here; I'm on the bus riding to school. And I'm not in danger at all. If only it didn't seem so *real!* If all my dreams are like this it's no wonder I never let myself remember them!

As if to remind herself just how impossible the whole thing was, Jennifer turned her head upward to look at the harpy. Sudden astonishment almost made her scream then, and again the question of dreaming was driven from her mind. For there, just above her, clung Samson, his face clenched with the strain of hanging on. A small sword hung at his waist and a coil of yellow rope, strangely shiny and smooth, was slung over his shoulder.

Jennifer was just about to cry out the dwarf's name but the look on his face stopped her. He wanted her to be silent. But why? Was it possible the harpy did not know he was there?

That Julia could not sense his grip seemed possible—brass feathers would not have much feeling in them. But what about the extra weight? Surely Julia would notice that! No, maybe not. She was strong, immensely so, even more than the other harpies. For her it would be like carrying two feathers instead of one; she could easily miss the difference.

But this was so frustrating! Jennifer longed to speak to Samson, to know if he had a plan. Incredibly, he was here, but she could say nothing for fear of giving his presence away. Had he and Prospero been able to work something out? What could it possibly be? Surely Swenhild's creatures would capture him as soon as they arrived at the castle, which was now close at hand. Samson would then have done nothing more than throw his life away along with hers.

The tears welled up in Jennifer's eyes once more. Poor Samson! she thought in anguish. And I thought he had let me down!

But now there was no time for further thought—the harpy was fast descending. The grim castle walls seemed to hurtle up to meet them in their flight and the harpy shrieked in triumph as she glided in low over the battlements.

The hideous wail drowned out Jennifer's own horrified scream, for just at that moment the small form of Samson plummeted past her and out of sight as they crossed over the castle wall close below. Apparently the dwarf had lost his grip at the last moment and had fallen to certain death upon the jagged rocks that ringed the castle on every side.

Jennifer was still sobbing broken-heartedly when the harpy set her down gently on the wide black stones of the roof. She watched through streaming eyes as the monstrous creature flew off again to take up a perch on the castle's tallest spire, and waited hopelessly for Swenhild to come and claim her.

It was not the witch herself who came, though,

but a pair of tall men in black clothing and black hoods that covered their faces. They did not speak but signalled Jennifer to rise and follow. With one marching before her and one behind, they crossed the roof to a narrow stairway leading down into the castle.

There were few comforts within. The worn stone passages were narrow and stuffy, decorated only by huge cobwebs where hideous spiders gobbled their prey and seemed to watch Jennifer's progress through their domain.

"Where are we going? Where are you taking me?" she asked more than once, but the only answer she received was the dying echo of her own trembling voice.

On and on the dimly lit passages wound, seemingly without end. More narrow staircases coiling down, always down; more forks and sudden turnings of the way; vast silent halls with vaulted roofs, empty of all life—such was the path that Jennifer trod, stumbling often now as terror robbed her limbs of strength.

Suddenly a cool breeze touched her face and the way broadened. More hooded figures joined them and marched along with them until they stood beneath the arched entrance to a mighty hall, mightier than any Jennifer had seen or even imagined—a domed and pillared cavern cut from the very rock of the cliff. One side was lined with tall, glassless windows, seven of them, that looked out over the sea. In all but one perched a harpy princess. Jennifer's heart stood still as the dreadful thought struck that the seventh window was meant for her.

She tore her eyes away and her gaze travelled across the vastness of the hall to a platform like an altar at the very centre of the floor. There stood Swenhild.

Jennifer knew it could be no one else, for in her and about her the many evils of the great castle seemed to have their focus. She was tall, taller than anyone Jennifer had ever seen, and she was straight and thin, and dressed in purple robes. In her old face glowed eyes like coals. They fixed on Jennifer in triumph, and held her in a gaze that pierced like pain and would not let her turn aside.

"Bind her!" hissed Swenhild softly. "Bring her to me!"

At once Jennifer was seized from behind by strong arms that bound her hand and foot with knots that dug painfully into her flesh. She was picked up and carried to the platform and left there writhing at Swenhild's feet.

"The Princess Miranda!" the sorceress rasped gloatingly.

"Greetings, my dear! Rinaldo has done well for me, I see. The witless fool! You are the seventh, the end of his promise to me. Soon it will be time for him to claim his reward. Ha! He shall have his reward, all right—his precious Kingdom of Eladeria! And he shall weep! Rinaldo, King of Waste, Lord of Ruin, Emperor of Ashes and Dust! Long may he reign to see the work we do, my Beauties and I!"

She waved a skinny hand to indicate the harpies, who shrieked deafeningly in reply. But it was Jennifer who broke the silence that followed.

"Is that all you want? To ruin Eladeria, to destroy it? Why? Why? It doesn't make any sense!"

Swenhild laughed, a sound softer but much more terrifying than the screaming of her Beauties.

"Because I choose to, child. Because it is my pleasure. For I am Swenhild, and my Song is a song of pain! You will hear it soon enough. You will serve me and fly for me, little Princess, and you will hate me even as you do my bidding! You will steal, yes, and kill at my command, with a cold roost and a slab of rotting meat for all your wages!"

"No!" protested Jennifer weakly. "I will not! I will not!"

"Believe me," hissed the sorceress, "you will!" She raised her voice slightly. "Take her!" she commanded. "To the Crystal Ring!"

Two hooded guards came forward. They dragged Jennifer to the far wall of the cavern so that Swenhild on her platform stood between her and the windows. Here the floor was marked with a strange pattern etched into the stone and bordered by a tall fence of clear crystal. There was a gate in the fence with hinges and lock of silver. The men quickly cut Jennifer's bonds and pushed her roughly through the gate, shutting it fast behind her.

She cast frantically about for some means of escape, but there was none. She ran from side to side of the wide cage, kicking at the crystal till it rang like a great bell, but it was strong and did not crack.

The harpies shrieked and the guards chuckled at her plight, but through it and above it all was the cackle of Swenhild's mocking laughter.

Now the sorceress began to sing and all other noises ceased. Her song had the sound of ancient, evil times, a melody to make the skin crawl, rising and falling in waves of malice and spite. Forbidden power crackled in the rancid air of the cavern as the song gathered strength, and Jennifer, on her knees and sobbing, felt the icy touch of magic on her brow.

No! she moaned to herself. No! This can't be happening! And then she straightened. It's now or never, she thought. I have to wake up! Samson is dead and in a moment I'll be—I have to get out of this dream *now!*

She shook her head violently, as if trying to shake loose the dream's grip on her mind. She pinched herself painfully on the cheeks and cried aloud, "Wake up! Wake up!"

It did no good. The dream, if it *were* a dream, went on and Swenhild's song grew stronger with each beat of Jennifer's thumping heart. She could feel something happening inside her, something strange and new, something so overpowering that she could only give herself up to it and weep.

And still the song went on.

12
The power of the Scroll

Samson sat on the sill of a small window, peering keenly into the dark passageway before him and waiting for his frantic heart to settle down. He did not like heights. Carefully he coiled the length of grapple-cord that Prospero had given him and slung it from a hook at his waist.

He looked again at the smooth yellow rope. It was amazing stuff. Soldiers had used it in the olden days, Prospero had said, when wizardry was stronger and such articles were commonplace. It would stick to anything, but it was made especially to stick to cold stone. There was nothing else like it for storming an enemy castle or for scaling a cliff. You just tossed up one end and it would stick fast and bear as much weight as the rope itself until you willed it to let go.

Samson had hardly believed that it would work, even when he threw himself desperately into the empty air as the harpy Julia crossed the outer parapets of Swenhild's castle, flinging the grapple-cord at the stone wall as he fell. Yet it had held, and the natural stretchiness of the rope had taken up much of the shock as he was suddenly brought up short at the other end. Then it had been a simple, if nerve-wracking, matter of working his way to a window, climbing hand over hand along the rope.

But there was no time to think of such things now. Samson dropped to his feet in the dim corridor and crept stealthily along it, seeking some sign that would lead him to Swenhild. He turned a corner, then suddenly pulled back. A guard!

Should he attempt to take the man by surprise, disarm him, force him to reveal where the sorceress was? No, it was just too risky. Samson was as strong as any ordinary man, but he lacked the size and reach to chance open combat.

He drew a dagger from his belt and dipped its point in a vial of Nevermind Water, Prospero's other gift to him. A moment later the guard went down noiselessly, the dagger protruding from his arm. He would be unconscious for hours, but he would recover. A good shot! Samson cleaned the dagger, then tore a strip from the guard's hood to bind the wound. This done, he went on.

Now a distant shrieking reached his alert ears. The harpies! Were they with Swenhild? It was a good bet that they were. To the left then, towards the sea. Samson's brows knit and he stole onwards, the dagger lying ready in his hand.

A few minutes later, with three more guards lying unconscious in the passages behind him, Samson drew near the great cavern. A shrill sound of singing made him shudder. He had heard its like before, yes, and had a score to settle! But what of Jennifer? He hurried on, hoping he was not too late.

In her crystal cage Jennifer had slumped to the stone floor and waited now for the changes to begin. How would it feel, what would it be like when her arms stretched slowly into broad wings, when her human legs dwindled and warped to become the clutching limbs of a bird, when Swenhild took command of her soul? She waited and felt the magic fill her, but nothing happened.

No, if anything she felt stronger than before. She clambered back to her feet to face the malice of Swenhild's song, and a small flame of hope began to flicker within her. A strange calm took possession of her mind; she was no longer very afraid. It was almost as though she had become someone else, someone other and greater than herself. Yet it was she and only she who put her hands against the crystal wall and lifted her eyes to meet the sorceress's gaze.

Still the song went on, but now at every note Jennifer felt new power mount within her—not hurting, not overcoming her, but clenching inside her like a mighty fist to strike back on her command. Suddenly she thought of Rinaldo's Spell of Tranquillity. Why had *it* not affected her? Could it be—Yes, that had to be the answer! The Paladian Scroll!

That strange design of multi-coloured lines. What had it done to her without her even knowing it? Magic could not harm her—even Swenhild's potent song was powerless against her now. Instead, the power used against her somehow became her own. She could feel it building every second!

Swenhild's song faded as the sorceress at last became aware that something was wrong. "Child!" she hissed venomously, and the sound of her voice was like poison in the air. "Child, what have you done?"

For answer Jennifer pressed her palms against the crystal, ever so lightly, and the cage shattered into a myriad of splinters that fell harmlessly all about her. She was light-headed, her blood racing in her veins, her body surging with stored-up power. She raised her outstretched hands towards the witch, and from her fingertips sprang a beam of spectral green light, straight at Swenhild's heart.

Swenhild barely saw the bolt in time. She leapt aside and the light splashed against the wall in a shower of sparks, melting and scarring the stone but harming no one. Still not fully understanding what was happening, the witch muttered under her breath and from her own hand unleashed a cloud of billowing fog, all deathly grey.

Like a living thing the cloud made noiselessly for Jennifer. She ran from it, not knowing what evil it held, but she could not evade it. Remorselessly it followed her and hemmed her in against a corner of the cavern, thickening and darkening in its flight. As it drew near her the cloud broke and became a swarm of furious, stinging wasps, not of any earthly kind but monstrous and magical, thirsting only for Jennifer's blood. The swarm closed on her face and bare arms and ankles, the sound of their buzzing growing louder and hungrier by the instant.

But then as each one settled on her skin and bit,

it vanished. The buzzing died and the only sound was Jennifer's laughter as she stepped forward once more into battle.

The guards had begun to advance, though very nervously, to form a wide ring about her that gradually tightened as they moved forward. Now at Swenhild's urging they came on faster, with a few of the braver ones brandishing daggers as they charged ahead of the rest.

Jennifer saw her danger, but she did not panic. She spun on her heels to face each guard in turn and aimed a pointing finger at each man's heart. One by one they tumbled to the ground unconscious, till at last only Swenhild and the watching harpies remained standing.

But the witch had not been idle. While Jennifer had been occupied with the guards, Swenhild had been singing another song, a Song of Weaving, with ruby light for thread and her own evil mind for a loom. She had woven a net, a strangling red net that she now cast towards Jennifer with a gleeful howl of triumph.

Jennifer went down rolling and wriggling as the net tightened about her, waiting for the surge of magic in her that would tell her she had absorbed its power. But nothing came and the net grew tighter still. Suddenly Jennifer knew why. The magic of the net was not directed *into* her, as the first song and the sting of the wasps had been, but *around* her, where it could not be altered by the enchantment of the Paladian Scroll.

"Squirm, dearie!" cackled Swenhild. "Grovel and squirm, for now you must die!"

The witch drew a dagger from a fold in her cloak and raised its curved and gleaming blade high above her head as she strode towards her helpless victim. But Jennifer still had power stored up from before and was not yet beaten.

"Not so, Wicked One!" she cried in a voice that was only half her own, and in that instant her body became a pale cloud, still with her own form but as thin as air itself. Like a puff of smoke she passed through the web of the witch's net and drifted some distance across the hall before she allowed herself to become solid once again.

Now Swenhild was truly enraged.

"After her, my Beauties!" she screeched. "After her! Scratch her, bite her, pluck out her eyes! Rip off her flesh and bring the clean bones to me! Fly, my Beauties, fly!"

With one voice the harpies screamed their hideous battle cry and launched themselves towards Jennifer. High above her head they climbed, grouping themselves into a wide circle like a great wheel. Then, on some unspoken signal they turned their pale girl-faces downward and swooped.

Jennifer hesitated, almost too long. She did not want to hurt them, but what choice did she have?

Wait! If Swenhild could control the harpies, why couldn't she? At least she had to try. Breathing deeply and summoning the last of her reserve of power, Jennifer bent her will to match Swenhild's own.

"Not me! *Not me!*" she shouted desperately as the harpies plummeted down. "It is Swenhild you hate, not me! It is she who made you what you are! Turn on her, turn on her! Do not let her win!"

At the last possible moment the harpies slowed their dive and began to wheel again, just above Jennifer, a look of doubt surfacing in their cold eyes.

"What's wrong with you?" shrieked Swenhild. "Kill her! *Kill her!* She is my enemy!"

"Yes! But I am not *your* enemy, Princesses!" cried Jennifer. "*She* is! Swenhild is your enemy! Resist her! Attack her! Cast her into the sea!"

Again the harpies moved as one. Their uncertainty was gone. They flew low, screaming their rebellion, and made a straight line for the sorceress.

But Swenhild did not falter. Her grating voice rose high in a new song and her hands did not tremble as she stretched them out to meet her peril.

Suddenly the harpies' screeching died and their wings failed them. One after another they tumbled unconscious to the floor, almost at the sorceress's feet. And now Jennifer could do no more than gape in mute amazement, for even as they lay there the harpies were changing.

Their brazen feathers seemed to melt and become silk robes. Their claws became hands and feet, their wings and stubby legs reshaped themselves into slender human limbs. Their hair softened, losing its harsh metallic sheen, and over their sleeping faces stole expressions of quiet peace.

There was no peace for Jennifer though. She stood panting, facing the witch defiantly, but she knew she had come to the end of her store of power. Whatever it was, whenever it came, Swenhild's next move would end the battle.

The sorceress knew it too. Her burning eyes seemed almost to flame as she put two skinny fingers to her lips and whistled shrilly. At once there was another rush of wings and the harpy Julia swooped down from her perch above the castle to answer her mistress's summons.

She flew into the cavern and wheeled to face Swenhild, awaiting the command to kill. Jennifer could no longer bear to look; she buried her face in her hands. She hoped that she would not suffer too much, but would die quickly.

"Take her!" hissed the witch. "Take her, my darling, and drop her into the sea! Feed her to the sharks, my lovely! Do it now!"

But Julia now saw for the first time the other Princesses stretched out sleeping on the floor in their human forms, saw the peace in their faces and knew how they had won it. Something happened in her spellbound mind; something broke free of Swenhild's chains.

She uttered a great cry of defiance, then sped at her old mistress so suddenly that the witch had barely time to throw herself to the ground to dodge the raking claws. Swenhild was back on her feet in a moment, though, and again she sang, though now her voice was feebler. She cast down her mightiest servant as she had the others, to lie insensible and take back her human shape.

Suddenly Swenhild felt something hit her from behind, knocking her flat on her face. It was Jennifer who, seeing her chance as the witch was occupied with the true Princess, had sprinted forward to tackle her, calling upon the last of her waning strength.

But Swenhild, old as she was, was tall and strong, and Jennifer was no match for her. The sorceress rose and lifted Jennifer easily in her arms and carried her kicking and struggling to the window. There she lifted her high up to hurl her into the sea.

"Now die!" Swenhild rasped. "Die and be forgotten! Die!"

At the same moment a coil of yellow rope snaked out from behind and wrapped itself around Jennifer's waist, and she felt herself being yanked back into the cavern. Her head struck hard on the stone floor, knocking her instantly unconscious, so she did not see the dagger that buried itself hilt-deep in Swenhild's back or hear the witch's cry as she fell headlong into the sea.

For a long moment there was no sound but the far-off screeching of gulls. Then came a groan, from the lips of a tall young man who had dropped to his knees not far from the window, and was now, with an effort of concentration, regaining his feet. He was clad in a green tunic belted with gold, and his black hair fell straight upon his shoulders. His handsome face wore an expression of dazed wonder as he surveyed the great chamber: the fallen guards, the sleeping Princesses and the end of the yellow rope still clutched in his right hand.

Suddenly he gave a cry and hastened to Jennifer's side, moving awkwardly as though uncertain of his balance. Shaking his head sadly he lifted her up in his arms and carried her over to where the Princess Julia lay still sleeping. He laid her gently there with her arms at her sides, then went in search of something to bind the gaping wound on her head. There was nothing more he could do for her.

13
After the battle

Jennifer lay on a bed of soft cushions in a spacious tent, tossing and turning in the grip of a high fever. Anxious attendants came and went, taking turns mopping her burning forehead with cool cloths or trying to get her to swallow the soft food they brought to her bedside.

Outside were other tents pitched on a meadow on the edge of a little village. It was evening. Horses grazed nearby, tired from a day of hard travel.

In Jennifer's tent was one who had hardly left her side for four long days. It was the tall young man who, after Swenhild's end, had bandaged the deep wound that now threatened Jennifer's life.

He turned to the pretty young girl beside him with eyes that glinted with fierce impatience. "What can Prospero be doing, Julia?" he demanded. "Stopping in every little hamlet to see the sights? He should have been here by now!"

"Peace, brother!" answered Princess Julia. "I am sure your friend is making all the speed he can. He is an old man and Tumbol would be a long ride from here even for you. And the messengers may have been delayed on their way."

"I know, I know!" grumbled Prince Corbold, for it was none other than he. "Still, if anything should happen to her . . . She saved us all, you know!"

"I do," replied his sister softly. "Who should know better than I? But you have done all you can, Corbold, and no one can ask more. Sleep now. I will wake you if there is news."

In truth Corbold had done a great deal. Following Swenhild's fall he had bandaged Jennifer's head and made her as comfortable as he could. Then he had set about trying to rouse the other Princesses, beginning with his sister Julia. It was not long until they were all awake, but none of them remembered anything that had happened after their arrival at Swenhild's lair. This was just as well, but it meant that Corbold had to do a great deal of explaining before he could make them understand.

By this time the guards were beginning to awaken also. At first the Prince was alarmed, but it soon proved that he had nothing to fear. Some of the guards had always been wicked, of course, and had served Swenhild willingly, but most were good men gathered by the harpies on their raids, whose minds the sorceress had enslaved to her will. The wicked ones ran off as soon as they learned that their mistress had been beaten, but the others did everything they could to help, for Swenhild's hold on them, like all her other enchantments, had ended with her plunge into the sea.

The castle was scoured rapidly for anything that

might prove useful. Rope, blankets, food, cooking utensils and many other articles Corbold required were quickly gathered. But the best find of all was a dozen black mares stabled deep within the castle, kept there for what foul purpose no one knew, but strong and well-tended all the same.

Then Corbold led them all from the castle, using a secret way he had discovered long before when he had escaped the witch's lair for the first time, and they assembled where the path opened onto a narrow strip of beach at the base of the cliff.

He assigned horses to seven of the Princesses, but Jennifer he put on a litter that could be carried easily by four walking men. Two of the horses he gave to men who were ill from long years of living on poor food in cramped, unhealthy quarters; the other three were loaded with food and supplies.

This still left a great deal to be carried in makeshift packs by those who went on foot, but Corbold got it organized at last and the party, numbering perhaps fifty, set off along the seashore in search of a road. It was still just midafternoon on the day after the Tribute.

Before nightfall they came to a highway and early the next morning, after a few hours of sleep under the stars, they reached their first town. The people there rejoiced when they heard of Swenhild's downfall, for they had often been raided by the harpies. They were happy to give Corbold every assistance they could.

Almost at once two of the townspeople, a man and a young woman known as skilled and swift riders, were enlisted as messengers. Corbold told them to go straight to Prospero and ask him to meet them on the highway as soon as possible, for he knew of no one else in the Kingdom who might have the skill to heal Jennifer's deadly wound. He instructed the messengers also to avoid the palace, and especially anyone connected with Rinaldo, but even so he had little doubt that the Chancellor would soon know that the Tribute had gone amiss.

When these and other arrangements had been made, Corbold prepared to leave. His party was smaller now, for many of the men decided to remain in the town and live there. Fresh horses were obtained, and a comfortable carriage for Jennifer, and it was not long before they could set off again.

That had been three days ago. Now the Prince slept at last on the floor of the tent while his sister tended to Jennifer with anxious care in her eyes. Even to one not skilled in healing it was clear that the ailing girl would soon be beyond help, for she had not wakened since her injury and her fever was mounting hourly.

Suddenly came the sound of galloping hooves that slowed as the horses drew nearer and finally halted nearby. Julia heard someone asking for directions and a moment later Prospero entered the tent, worry shadowing his old face. Corbold was already on his feet.

"Prospero, old friend!" he cried gladly, embracing the old man. "Thank goodness you are here!"

Prospero looked startled for a moment, then he peered closely at the young Prince as though searching for something in his face. Finally he bowed.

"Forgive me," he said carefully, "but I do not

recollect ever having met your Highness before."

"No, of course you haven't," smiled Corbold. "How foolish of me! But come, Prospero, at least you know the Princess Miranda. She is gravely sick and it may be that even you cannot help her. But you must try. And spare no effort, for she has saved me and my sister—yes, and the Kingdom itself."

Prospero nodded.

"So I have been told," he answered. "Well, I will do what I can."

He went to Jennifer's side and knelt there, staring at her for a time without touching her. Then he picked up her hand, held it in his own and muttered something in a voice too soft for the others to hear.

At once Jennifer's breathing, which had been fast, shallow and irregular, eased and became more steady, while some of the flush faded from her cheeks.

"It is well that I did not delay," Prospero said. "Another hour even and I might have been too late. But I think she will recover. I will need herbs, your Highness, and certain berries that I think may be found near this place. Oh yes, and I will need wine, a good deal of it."

"Wine?" asked Corbold in a puzzled tone. "Surely it would not be good to give her wine?"

"The wine is for me, your Highness," smiled Prospero weakly. "I am little used to hard riding."

Corbold laughed aloud.

"It shall be as you say, my friend!" he exclaimed. "But come, make out a list of the other things you require and they shall be sent for at once. I myself shall bring you wine."

People were soon dispatched, under Princess Julia's direction, to collect Prospero's medicines. Even before they returned, though, Jennifer opened her eyes sleepily. The first thing she saw was the old man's gentle face looking down on her.

"Prospero!" she said feebly. "Can it really be you? Then I'm not–not–"

"Dead? No," answered Prospero, "though you have been nearer death than most others now living. But you are getting better."

"Then it's all right?" asked Jennifer. "I mean, with Swenhild and everything? Is *she* dead?"

"It is all right," Prospero assured her. "As to whether Swenhild is dead, who can say? A sorceress is not easily killed. But she *is* beaten. You have beaten her and it may well be that she will never rise again. But rest now, Jennifer. Sleep. There will be time in the morning to talk of these things."

"One more question," begged Jennifer, "and then I'll sleep, I promise. I am so tired. Samson, where is he? I think it must have been he who saved me. Is he all right? Did he–Oh, and who are you?"

Prince Corbold had come forward just then to kneel beside Prospero. He looked down on Jennifer with a glad smile, but his face quickly became serious again.

"Samson is no more," he said softly. "You will never see him again, Jennifer."

Tears started at once in Jennifer's eyes.

"Never see him again? You mean he's dead? Oh, Samson, Samson!"

Jennifer began to sob but Corbold said, "No, he is not dead."

She stared at him without understanding until Prospero spoke. "Samson was not born a dwarf, Jennifer. That was the form Swenhild put upon him in revenge and mockery when he sought to save his sister. She changed him into a dwarf and dressed him as a jester. After his escape from her lair he returned to the palace with a new name and bided his time until he could revenge himself on her for Julia's sake, and for his own. This is Prince Corbold, returned again to his true form."

Jennifer's eyes widened, but not so wide as Corbold's.

"Then you knew all along, my sly old friend!" he exclaimed. "You knew it all already!"

"Knew or guessed," nodded the old man. "But I guessed also your reasons for keeping your true identity to yourself. If Rinaldo had ever found out who you really were we may be sure he would have stopped at nothing to be rid of you."

"Rinaldo!" exclaimed Jennifer. "I had almost forgotten about him! What do you think he will do now?"

"That we shall soon see," Prospero said. "But it is late and you must rest, Jennifer. Let Rinaldo wait until the morning." He touched her lightly on the cheek with his forefinger and she fell at once into a sound sleep.

14
Theobald the King

By morning Jennifer felt already so much better that she was able to walk to the carriage by herself. Prospero, who had wakened her several times during the night to make her drink his healing potions, rode with her, as did Princess Julia.

With Jennifer out of danger, Corbold was able to turn his mind to what they would do when they arrived at the palace. He rode now on horseback, impatient with every delay and often going ahead to scout the countryside for possible dangers.

There was no trouble along the way, however, and it was not long after sundown that day that the party rode in through the palace gate and up to the wide steps. Corbold and most of his men went ahead while Jennifer and the other Princesses came behind with Prospero and a handful of guards.

When they got inside it was clear that Rinaldo had gathered his forces for an all-or-nothing final stand. He stood on one side of the Great Hall with a crowd of heavily armed men around him, while on the other side was ranged the rest of the palace household, nobles and commoners both. They bore only what few weapons they had been able to lay their hands on, for Rinaldo alone controlled the palace armoury.

At the head of those loyal to the King stood old Duke Hugo and Dame Isobel, he with his sword drawn, she awkwardly holding an oaken staff. There was no doubt that if it came to a fight Rinaldo and his men would be the winners.

Into this scene strode Corbold, his sword also drawn. A hush fell on the gathering as one by one people recognized him. Tall and commanding, he stopped in the middle of the Hall and faced Rinaldo sternly.

"Duke Rinaldo," he cried in a loud voice, "I, Corbold, Prince of Eladeria, command thee to lay down thine arms and give thyself up to the justice of the King! Obey if thou would have mercy!"

"Begone, stripling Prince!" retorted Rinaldo. "I know well what mercy I should have of you! Begone! The Kingdom is mine! I seize it now and you will not prevent me!"

So saying he came forward with his men close around him, and in that instant the Hall became a battlefield. Corbold and those of his people who were armed were hard pressed from the start, being outnumbered at least two to one. They fought valiantly, though, and the fighting went on for some time without either side gaining a clear advantage over the other.

At last Rinaldo's greater numbers and superior weapons began to tell and Corbold's band was slowly driven back into a corner of the hall, their final defeat now only a matter of time.

Suddenly Prospero, who with the Princesses had been watching from one side, leaned over and whispered in Jennifer's ear.

She nodded. "Yes, I think it would work! Try it, Prospero, and hurry!"

Prospero began to chant the same potent Spell of Healing that he had used on Jennifer the night before, but this time she was stronger and did not need its magic for herself. The enchantment of the Paladian Scroll was still upon her and she felt herself once again alive with its power. She stepped forward towards the battle.

It was not little Jennifer the awestruck onlookers saw, but a giantess twice the height of the tallest there, for so she made herself appear. Suddenly the battle ceased to rage; all eyes were turned on her.

"Rinaldo," she cried in a terrible voice, "your hour has come!"

She stretched out her hand towards the astonished Chancellor and there was a chorus of horrified screams as he burst suddenly into flames that blazed briefly and went out, leaving no more than a heap of cinders on the floor.

"Who will be next?" cried Jennifer. "You?"

One of Rinaldo's stupider men had taken it into his head to rush her with his sword. Jennifer waved her hand again and this man too was instantly aflame.

That was enough. The rest could not hurl down their weapons quickly enough as they threw themselves on the floor and begged for mercy. Corbold's followers rushed in at once to gather up the fallen weapons, and none too soon. Jennifer's power was exhausted and she was again a little girl.

Now it could be seen that Rinaldo and the other man were not burned to cinders after all, but only sleeping soundly on the floor. One of Corbold's men roused them, none too gently, with the point of his sword; like the other rebels they were bound and placed under guard.

With the fighting over, those of Corbold's people who were not guarding the prisoners or tending those who had been wounded in battle broke into a din of excited chatter. They were so busy congratulating each other, and Cobold and Julia, and especially Jennifer, that at first no one noticed the old man who now walked stiffly and slowly into the Hall. He wore a rich robe and had a staff clutched in one hand for support. A golden crown perched on his snowy head.

Onward he came to the middle of the Hall until one by one the people saw him and fell silent. In a few moments the clamour of voices had ceased; then a rousing cheer arose from the crowd. Everyone watched with joy as first Princess Julia and then Prince Corbold came forward to hug their father and stand by him. The adopted Princesses stood awkwardly to one side, hardly knowing what to do or where to look until Corbold called them forward to stand with the King. Even then only Jennifer was bold enough actually to hug the old man.

Then Rinaldo was brought before the King. Seeing that there was no hope of further resistance, the Chancellor threw himself down on his knees.

"Your Majesty," he began, "my heart is glad to see you at last out of bed! I trust you are not too tired, my Liege."

The King's voice was weak but stern and unwavering as he replied, "Oh, I am very tired, Rinaldo. But I sensed that Swenhild was overthrown, for the power of your spells has diminished. My strength has been returning and I think I shall be feeling much better soon. Unlike you, Rinaldo!"

"I fear your Majesty's ears have been poisoned by idle gossip," Rinaldo whined. "Your Majesty's health has ever been my greatest concern!"

"The destruction of my health, you mean!" snapped the King. "But come, I have no patience for this! Duke Rinaldo, I now speak your doom! At this moment you are stripped of your title, of your duties, of your lands and all other properties, and I now pronounce upon you and all your followers the sentence of banishment from my realm for seven years and seven days from this day. Do not expect mercy should you return before that term. Now begone!"

Rinaldo did not bow or even look at the King as he slunk from the Hall by a side door. Corbold motioned some of the guards to follow and ensure that he did not escape custody, for his bonds had been removed before his audience with the King. When this was done the King turned to Corbold, smiling. Already long years seemed to have fallen from him, for his back was unbent and his eyes were as bright as the Prince remembered them from days long past.

"Come, my son," he said gaily. "And you, my

daughter. That is," he added after a moment, "my daughters, I should say. Goodness, what a lot of you there are! Did ever a King have so many daughters, I wonder? All of you come. We have so much to talk about, don't we? For one thing, Corbold, we have to choose a new Chancellor. There is much to be put back in order, I am sure, much of Rinaldo's mischief to be undone. Who shall take on this task for us?"

"I think I know of one who might do, Sire," said Corbold.

"You do?" The King looked rather surprised. "Well, for someone who's been away for seven years you certainly take hold of things quickly, Corbold! Whom do you have in mind?" His voice dropped to a whisper. "I say, you don't mean old Hugo, do you, my boy? Hugo's a good fellow and as loyal as anyone, but I don't think—"

"No, Sire," laughed the Prince, "not Duke Hugo. I think he is quite happy in his present position. The man I have in mind is not one of the palace household but a scroll-seller from the town. His name is Prospero."

The King was astonished.

"A scroll-seller! A commoner, Corbold? Are you thinking quite clearly, my son?"

"Quite clearly, Sire. A commoner Prospero may be, but he is the wisest person I know, save only yourself. And Rinaldo's Dukedom is vacant now: Prospero need not *remain* a commoner."

"That is so," said the King thoughtfully. "But where is this man you speak of so highly? Is he here?"

Corbold signalled for Prospero to come forward.

"Your Majesty?" he said, kneeling to Theobald.

"My son here wants me to make you a Duke, sir," the King said. "*And* Lord High Chancellor. What do you say to that?"

If Prospero hadn't been on his knees he would probably have fallen over. But in a moment he collected himself again and replied, "I crave your Majesty's pardon, but I am happy in my present life. I am too old a dog for such new tricks, your Majesty, and I fear I must respectfully decline the honour Prince Corbold would do me."

Oh, Prospero! thought Jennifer vexedly. How could you? It would be just the thing for you.

But the King did not look pleased.

"I am an older dog than you, sir!" he exclaimed. "Be careful what you say! And as for declining, that is for me to decide, not you!"

"I-I beg your Majesty's forgiveness!" stammered Prospero. "I intended no disrespect. I meant only that I have too little experience with affairs of state to do justice to such a high office, and I urgently recommend that your Majesty find someone more suitably qualified."

"Very well," said Theobald. "That settles that."

Prospero rose to take his leave.

"Just a moment," the King said sharply. "I didn't tell you to leave. Kneel again! Yes, that's better. Prospero, scroll-seller of Tumbol, arise Duke Prospero, Lord High Chancellor of Eladeria. There. That wasn't so bad, was it?"

"B-b-but, your Majesty!"

"Peace, my Lord Duke. Remember this, Corbold,

when you are King," Theobald went on, turning to his son. "If somebody *wants* a job like the Chancellor's, with all the power and all the worry that go with it, better not give it to him! Now come, all of you! I'm getting tired with so much standing around. Let us go someplace more comfortable. Tonight we talk; tomorrow we feast! Come!"

15
Prospero's Gift

The King was true to his word, except that the feast went on for three days rather than one. The merriment spread from the palace out into the town and across the countryside until all of Eladeria was caught up in the celebration. Hugo outdid himself as usual, and was so happily busy that he barely had time to snatch a bite or two of his own banquet.

On the fourth day the feasting came to an end and the long work of repairing seven years of mischief had to begin. There was little place in this labour for the seven adopted Princesses. At first they found plenty to do just strolling about the palace grounds, petting the animals and talking to the gardeners, or making trips into the town and about the countryside in the splendid carriages furnished for them by the King.

At last, though, they longed to be back in their own world, to see their families and their friends, to wake up from their long dreaming. So Jennifer went to Prospero, now very busy and important in his work as Chancellor, and asked him if he knew of any way to undo the spell that had brought the girls to Eladeria.

Prospero smiled and rummaged amongst his stack of royal proclamations and documents of state, until at length he found a dusty scroll.

"I found this in Rinaldo's library a few days ago," he said. "I think it contains the spell you need—a Spell of Returning. I do not know if I have the power to make it work, but I will try if you and the others wish me to."

Jennifer nodded somewhat sadly and said, "If you have the time, dear Prospero. We do not belong here, you know, though it will be hard to leave you and all our other friends."

"I understand," he told her. "And it will be hard to lose you, above all, Jennifer, who have done so much to aid us. I wish only that there was something we could do for you in return. Is there? Is there some gift or service that would please you? If so, only speak and if it can be done it will be."

"Oh, Prospero," answered Jennifer, "what more can you give me than you have already, without my asking? I don't need—" She broke off suddenly as a curious thought struck her. "Wait a moment though. Do you suppose . . . "

She explained her idea to Prospero and the old man chuckled and nodded his head.

"A strange request!" he exclaimed. "Yet I rather think it can be done. A very little spell should serve—not beyond even my small power. Very well, Jennifer, I shall see that it is done!"

The next day the entire household gathered in

the Great Hall at midmorning, from the King himself down to the lowliest stableboy. There were speeches and music and many farewells, but at last Prospero stepped into the centre of the gathering, a staff in his left hand and a long scroll in his right.

The adopted Princesses came forward too, to stand in a half-circle before him. They were wearing the clothes they had worn when they first arrived in Eladeria. These had been carefully laid by and stored at Rinaldo's command—a prize to prove the power he wielded even in another world, thanks to the evil magic of Swenhild. Very strange and out of place the girls looked in their everyday garments, which no longer seemed everyday to them. But Prospero bowed to them courteously, and at a nod from King Theobald he began to chant.

On and on his incantation went, so long that Jennifer began to wonder if the old man really didn't have enough power to make the Spell of Returning work. Then there was a little flash of light and a sharp sound rather like a door closing, and the Princess Celinda, who had been the first of the seven to arrive, abruptly vanished. There was a gasp from the assembly and Jennifer felt a cold tingling at the back of her neck, but Prospero's chanting did not cease.

One after another the nervous Princesses disappeared. Clarissa was next, then Amelia, Amaranth, Violet and Tara. Finally only the Princess Miranda remained, Jennifer alone with every eye upon her.

Prospero paused. Jennifer looked questioningly at him and he nodded gently and said, "Yes, you may have a minute more. But no longer."

Gladly Jennifer rushed over to King Theobald, who was quite affected at so suddenly losing so many of his large family. She hugged him and kissed him on the cheek as she had done once before. He looked like a King again now—tall and straight, with clear eyes and fewer lines on his face than there had been.

She ran next to Corbold, who bent down to kiss her forehead and said smilingly, "A happy awakening to you, Jennifer! You must have slept long!"

"Goodbye, Samson!" Jennifer said. "Please don't go hunting anymore!"

Then to Julia, Duke Hugo, Dame Isobel and Prospero, each in turn. Jennifer hugged them all and said goodbye for the last time. Then she returned to her place in front of Prospero.

As the old man began chanting again she felt the familiar sensation of power growing in her body and knew that if she chose she could use it for any purpose she desired, thanks to the magic of the Paladian Scroll. But now she only wanted to be home, so she stood calmly with closed eyes and let Prospero's spell do its work.

She was suddenly startled by a babble of chattering voices. She opened her eyes in surprise, fearing that something had happened to interrupt the working of the spell.

Nothing had.

She was back on the schoolbus, still climbing the long hill up from the bridge. The chattering was that of her friends.

"Look, everybody!" shouted Carol from across the aisle. "Jennifer's smiling! She must be feeling sick or something!"

Jennifer laughed with everyone else. It felt good to be back.

Then she noticed her satchel, which was across her lap as usual, with all her books and papers in it. It reminded her of something and she opened it. Right at the top of the things piled inside she found three sheets of paper covered from top to bottom with writing in her own hand, though a good deal neater than usual.

At the top of the first page were the words *My Strangest Dream.*

I dreamt that I had been captured by a powerful witch, Prospero's gift began, *who put me in a cage of solid crystal. But though she did not know it, in my dream I had a strange power of my own.*

Then came the tale of the battle and a little of what happened after. The story finished with: *And so I awoke in my own world, still thinking of my dear friends, especially of the wise old Prospero who had been so kind to me. But was it a dream or wasn't it?*

The End.